THE ROYAL CONQUEST

Scandalous House of Calydon

THE ROYAL CONQUEST

Scandalous House of Calydon

STACY REID

Entangled Publishing, LLC
2614 South Timberline Road
Suite 109
Fort Collins, CO 80525
Visit our website at www.entangledpublishing.com.

Scandalous is an imprint of Entangled Publishing, LLC.

Edited by Alycia Tornetta
Cover design by Erin Dameron-Hill
Cover art from iStock and PeriodImages

Manufactured in the United States of America

First Edition November 2015

SCANDALOUS

For my nephew, Alexander Westcarr

Chapter One

OCTOBER, 1883
ENGLAND, NORFOLK, SHERRING CROSS

The thief smelled exotically alluring—sweet, feminine, an elusive whisper of spiced wine and strawberries. Very much at odds with the tightly fitted trousers, billowing white shirt, and cap the person wore. The shadows shifted in the prodigious Calydon stables, and the interloper slinked forward, moving with the elegance of a sensual feline.

A woman. Without any doubt. Only an imbecile would ever imagine those delightful curves belonged to a young man, despite the mode of dress. She strode forward, the strong breeze lifting her shirt, baring to his eyes the delectable curve of her mouth-watering rump. The shadows dipped, and she disappeared with the darkness. Why was she creeping about around the stables in the dead of night? A maid meeting her lover for a tryst? With her clandestine approach, it was more likely for her to be doing something underhanded. Who would be so bold as to sneak into the Duke of Calydon's property to steal one of his prized stallions?

Mikhail moved with the silent grace of a predator, using his sharpened senses, honed from being a grand general in the Russian Army, to track the woman, not even a whisper of sound betraying his movements. Shrouding himself in the pockets of darkness, he wove through the stalls, listening to the soft footfall of the intruder.

There was a rustle of sound, a sharp inhalation of what could be appreciation…or desire.

"You beautiful, magnificent beast. I want to ride you so desperately," a low husky voice crooned. "I want to feel your power and strength between my thighs. Will you allow me to mount you?"

Sweet merciful Christ.

Mikhail's body reacted with painful immediacy to the woman's words. The softly purring voice stoked his intrigue. Suddenly, irrationally, he wanted to be the one to be ridden, hard and desperately by this faceless female. Absurd to be sure, for he was not a man to be led around by his cock…*ever*. He had always selected his lovers with utter discretion and only succumbed to pleasures of the flesh after conversing at length with a potential bedmate. Not to mention conducting a thorough investigation into her background. He assuredly did not jump into meaningless encounters, no matter how tempting. He had more control over his desires than that, especially after his days of torment under Madam Anya. Yet with innocent words, this unknown woman had his mouth drying and lust rising hot and thick inside him.

"Will you allow me to ride you? *Please* allow me… I need to feel you underneath me," she purred.

A sharp neigh sounded, and a throaty laugh spilled into the air. "It seems as if we are in agreement." Her murmur was filled with awe and triumph.

Moonlight sliced through the darkness of the vast stables,

and he was able to make out her form as she stopped at his horse Sage's stall. She moved with liquid grace as she eased closer to the massive black horse. Stallions were considered unsuitable mounts for young ladies, yet she seemed determined to ride Sage. Mikhail wondered if he should speak, but he dismissed the idea. He was too enthralled by the unconventionality playing before him. She roused his interest, a curious change from the bitter desolateness and icy disdain that had shrouded his heart for years.

Who is she?

A thief? If so, she picked the wrong night to pilfer from the Calydon stables. She opened the latch to the stall, all the while crooning sweet nonsense. Sage seemed to lap it up, because Mikhail's damn temperamental stallion allowed her closer, nickering his welcome, nudging her shoulders playfully. With an efficiency and strength that was surprising, she saddled Sage and fitted his reins.

Definitely not a novice.

Using the mounting block, she seated herself atop the horse with supreme confidence, no hesitation or fear displayed at the sheer size of the beast beneath her. She sighed, stretched, and then pouting lips, the only visible part of her face, curved into an irresistibly alluring smile.

An intense jolt of lust hardened Mikhail's length with such swiftness that for a heartbeat he felt light-headed. *What the hell is this?* Must be the vodka he had drunk earlier. It was the only explanation for his lack of restraint over his desires. His heart pounded, and he breathed evenly, controlling his body's startling reaction to such raw sensuality.

Thunder rumbled and light flashed across the sky. Sage did not shift, but she gripped his reins tighter, glancing through the massive open slat windows into the night. Mikhail could smell the storm in the air, feel the vibrations of the thunder. *Do not leave*, he urged silently. He did not want to have to track her down, and until he chose to make his presence known to London society it was best to keep a low profile. Mikhail certainly did not want Princess Tatiana Ivanovna tracking him to England to plead her case. God save him from perfidious females. But most importantly he wanted—no, he needed—some peace before wading back into the fray of society. He doubted revealing his presence to this unknown woman would compromise his plan, but caution still curled inside him.

He shuffled a foot, hoping to startle the young lady into abandoning whatever reckless plan she possessed. She froze, her head twisting toward where he stood in the dark. Mikhail held himself still, waiting for her move, waiting for feminine nerves to overtake her. After worrying her bottom lip with her teeth, she spun the horse toward the entrance and took off.

He smiled and moved in the shadows, careful to remain hidden in the event she turned around. Another crack of thunder and he glanced skyward. There was no doubt a storm was brewing. Was she familiar with the terrain, and did she know where the cottages were on the Calydon property? The storm clouds in the sky gathered, and he cursed himself for caring about a stranger.

Mikhail moved unhurriedly to the entrance. It was easy to make out her form under the banner of moonlight. She rode like a dream. Her laughter floated on the wind, and he hated to ruin her enjoyment, but he could not allow her to steal his stallion. He placed his fingers against his lips and let a sharp whistle rent the air, then cursed as a boom of thunder hid the signal that would have caused Sage to return to Mikhail despite her urgings. He quickly readied another horse. It was damn reckless of him to follow the female, even if she was a thief, but he felt compelled to pursue her.

"Allow me to follow the woman. I will return your prized

stallion, Prince Alexander," a low voice said to his left.

He glanced at Vladimir, Mikhail's friend and constant shadow. "You forget my instructions. You will refer to me as Mikhail until I say otherwise."

There was a pulse of silence and he could feel Vladimir's disapproval, but Mikhail would not be swayed on this.

"You are not being yourself, you do not chase women, even if they are unusual and provocative, Mikhail."

The last was uttered with grudging respect. And Mikhail would admit he was being a touch hasty, but it was a truth he was willing to ignore. "You will not follow me."

"I will—"

At his pointed stare, Vladimir paused, executed a sharp bow, and melted into the darkness.

Mikhail launched himself onto one of Calydon's stallions and surged from the stable.

He was *chasing* her.

Mayhap it could be that he'd allowed Calydon to goad him to drink brandy to test its potency against Mikhail's vodka. The combination must have done something to his hard-won discipline, because the sharp interest that pierced him even now was unsettling. He was pursuing the unknown woman more for the desire to learn her identity than to recover his horse. His actions were so unlike him. He should be treading with caution; instead he was being reckless.

A blasted foolish thing to do.

Eagerness churned inside of Miss Payton Peppiwell, and a rare smile of peace tilted her lips. Cold filled her lungs as she inhaled the brisk air. She would ride the wind this morning. "Go, my beauty," she crooned as she nudged the side of the massive stallion, encouraging him to move faster, reveling in the sheer power and grace of the animal.

After colliding with the Honorable Lord Jensen St. John earlier in the village, everything had been off-kilter. Payton had believed she'd forgiven him. But the surge of rage and pain she had felt at his renewed declarations stunned her.

I must not think of him.

Thunder rumbled in the distance, and she frowned. She hoped it would not rain. Riding was one of her joys in life, and she craved an outlet for all the emotions roiling through her, to feel the bunch and release of muscle between her thighs, the sheer power of the magnificent horse as they raced across the plains. That was why she had chosen one of the duke's stallions to mount, and not one of his gentle mares young ladies were encouraged to ride.

She rose before the rest of the household, determined to be free for at least a few hours before fielding the demands of her mother and her aunt, the Countess of Merryweather, to find a rich and titled husband.

Payton would enjoy her early morning adventure, and she would *not* think of her family's persistent pressure or Lord Jensen's renewed sentiments. As if mocking her, his words crowded her mind.

I have been a blasted fool, Payton. Forgive me. I beseech you to marry me.

His offer no longer held any enticement. There was a time when she had longed for the social whirl of the society. Curious and intrigued by the power the *haute monde* held, she'd desperately wanted to be a part of their selective world. She had danced too close to the flames and she had been burned, jilted by a man she had believed adored her, as he'd ardently professed. His actions had turned society's unpleasant and hurtful scorn in her direction. Her broken engagement had filled most of high society, if not all, with delight. An American miss who had dared to try and elevate herself with one of their beloved lords had been firmly reminded of her place.

Her sister Phillipa had warned Payton of the fickleness and the hypocritical nature of those who belonged to the highest echelon of society, but she had not believed. She'd been too enthralled by the excitement of attending lavish balls, picnics, and carriage rides. Though she had still been on the fringe, as an American with no ties to nobility, capturing the interest of the honorable Jensen St. John, heir to the Viscounty of Kenilworth, had been a sweet and thrilling coup.

He had been so friendly and obliging, always seeking her company. After weeks of walking out together and dancing at least once at every ball she had attended, St. John had proposed. He was a charming and very affable young man, and Payton had said yes to his offer without hesitation. And all it had taken for him to shatter her was the spreading of a rumor about her soon to be brother-in-law, Lord Anthony Thornton's bastardy.

Payton closed her eyes against the bittersweet memory, grateful she had not been seduced into giving Lord Jensen her chastity. Now that the *haute monde* had been unsuccessful in crushing the Calydon bastards—as Lord Anthony and his kindhearted sister, Constance, now the Duchess of Mondvale—had been referred to, Lord Jensen must believe the disdain Payton had been shown by association would melt away.

How could he imagine she would welcome him back into her life and heart?

"I will not be made a fool of again, and I will never allow my heart to be bruised by another lord." Her vow was snatched away by the icy wind.

With a jerk, the wind tugged the cap from her head, loosening the knot she'd tied her hair in. But she did not pause, reveling in the sheer freedom of her ride. A boom of thunder echoed across the land, and she drew on the reins, slowing the horse. "Easy," she crooned, rubbing the nape of his neck as he reared at another rumble.

The sky had darkened, eclipsing the stars, and she could now smell the rain on the air. She spun the horse around, startled to realize she had been so lost in her thoughts, she had ridden farther than she intended. Payton stirred uneasily in the saddle as she made out a lone figure in the distance, also on horseback.

Who else would be up and about at this hour?

The first drop of rain splashed on her cheeks. *Drat.* She would not make it back to the main house before the deluge. Turning her horse in a sharp move, she nudged him toward a cottage in the far distance. She recognized the area surrounding it as the hunting grounds of the Calydon property. Was it a hunting cottage? Not that it mattered, she only needed a suitable shelter until the worst of the rain passed, then she could slip back to the main estate without being seen.

A fork of lightning split the sky and slammed into the ground. Sparks flew from the earth, and the stallion reared. Payton desperately tried to prevent her fall, hooking her legs into the stirrups. She failed abysmally. The breath rushed from her lungs as her body made the hard impact with the ground. Her landing was bone-jarring. She tried to stand, and nausea churned in her stomach. The sky opened, and it started to rain fat, cold drops. Within seconds she was trembling. Stumbling to her feet, she lurched forward and then crumpled, collapsing on the grass.

Chapter Two

Payton's eyes fluttered open to see a dark angel hovering over her, concern etched in his shockingly handsome features. She shifted, and a moan slipped from her, alerting him to her conscious state. His gaze flew to hers, and her chest constricted. *Glorious heavens.* His eyes were the darkest blue of midnight—magnificent and distressingly sinful.

"Oh," slipped from her lips, before she had the presence of mind to contain her visceral reaction to such a fine pair of eyes.

The stranger's gaze caressed her form, and a sensual smile tilted the corner of his lips.

"Hello," he said in a slow drawl that rippled over her skin with awareness. "I am Mikhail Konstantinovich. I saw you fall from the horse and brought you here for shelter since the main house was too far to travel in your state. I attended to you to the best of my capabilities."

He had the most unique accent. One she had never heard before, but its husky dulcet tone sank into her body, stirring tantalizing heat.

I've gone mad.

She vaguely remembered the pain of landing in an undignified heap on her backside, the brutal cold of the rain and winds, powerful arms lifting her, the sensation of being on a horse, then someone removing her sodden tunic and trousers and tenderly drying her skin. Though a fire in the brazier warmed the room, a chill enveloped Payton.

He removed my clothes.

With a raw gasp, she lurched upright. She was swaddled in a blanket, but she could feel she was completely naked beneath. *Naked!* Payton swayed, her body trembled in reaction to the knowledge, and she felt certain she would expire from the shock.

I will not faint.

"Where are my clothes?" Her pulse hammered, and her knuckles ached from gripping the blanket too tightly. "Please get back," she snapped, fear making her voice husky.

He rose from his crouch in front of her and his long-legged stride carried him swiftly across the room, where he sprawled by the fire in an armchair, but his piercing eyes never left her face. It was an illusion, but she felt better with the short distance.

His black hair was wet, and his white shirt was plastered to the wall of his chest, and with each movement the muscle rippled and twisted with grace. Was he not cold? She could still feel the chill from the raging storm outside.

"Are you hurt anywhere? I felt no broken bones, but that does not mean there was no injury."

He felt *no broken bones*. It was impossible to hold back the sharp tremor of uncertainty that quivered through her. "Did you check for injuries before or after you undressed me?" Everything in Payton screeched to a halt when the words barreled from her mouth. Painful heat scorched her cheeks. The situation was so unusual and mortifying.

"I had the presence of mind to do so before I undressed you."

Was it her imagination his voice had gone huskier?

"Where are you hurt?" The concern in his tone was evident, but mistrust sliced through Payton. She tensed and then stifled a moan. Her body felt stiff, and there was a throbbing ache along her left hip, but no serious pain. *Thank heavens.*

"Are you a doctor?"

A decidedly imperious brow rose. "No."

She scowled. "Are you related in any way to a profession that would deem it suitable for you to examine my person?"

His lips twitched, and she wanted to growl. The maddening man found her amusing, when the situation called for anything but humor. A disaster of the scandalous and unrecoverable type loomed on the horizon.

"No," he finally answered.

"Then I am not hurt, thank you."

"I am relieved you are not injured. I mean you no harm, Lady…"

Her wariness must have been apparent, yet he looked at her expectantly. Payton almost snorted. As if she would reveal her identity. She sat up fully on the edge of the narrow but well-padded bed, clutching the blanket to her throat as if it were a lifeline. The stone floor beneath her bare feet was cold, and she barely prevented herself from acting too jittery.

She needed her wits about her, and it was crucial for her to appear unafraid. "I must warn you, Mr. Konstantinovich, I know how to fight, *very* well." She narrowed her gaze in what she hoped was a sufficiently threatening manner. "So I caution you to keep your distance while I go about my business, or else you will sorely regret it."

Surprise flashed across his features, then a smile of possibly admiration lifted his lips. He held out his arms in a non-threatening manner, as if a man so darkly handsome and intimidating, with the grace and power with which he had moved, could be innocuous. Of what sort of man was she at the mercy?

He regarded her with an obvious amusement that irked her.

"I am a guest and friend of the Duke of Calydon. I was in the stables when you entered. I thought you might have been a thief, absconding with my prize stallion. I followed, and I witnessed your need."

She stiffened, searching his face, probing and assessing. "I am no thief, and your assumption is offensive, sir. I, too, am a guest. What is most suspicious is you being in the stables at four in the morning. If there were a thief…it certainly was not *me*."

The blasted man laughed, and the sound was so rich and masculine, it caressed her senses with wicked allure.

"I was bedding down in the loft, and I was not the one skulking around."

"*I* was most certainly not skulking around. Ladies do not skulk," she gritted out.

A friend of the duke was bedding down in the stables?

He frowned thoughtfully and then gave a firm nod, answering whatever question plagued him. "No…it was skulking."

Arghh. Why was she allowing him to nettle her so, when the most important matter had not been addressed? "Where are my clothes, sir?"

Payton did not enjoy being so brusque, but it was impossible to pretend politeness. All of the lessons in decorum her aunt had relentlessly instructed seemed silly in this moment. She certainly could not remember any deportment lessons on what to do if one found oneself naked with a strange man in a remote cottage. Actually, if her memory served, she was supposed to scream, possibly swoon, and if he were rich and titled she should do all in her power to ensure they were compromised. She snorted in the most unladylike manner, and a dark brow lifted in question. As if his casual display of arrogance would prompt her to share her private thoughts.

A quick glance around the cabin did not reveal her garments. "My clothes, if you please, sir." She controlled the wince at her acerbic tone. Though she didn't need to contain her reaction, the blasted man remained unflappable at her ire. Most gentlemen would excuse themselves, not stare at her with such shivering intensity.

"They were soaked, and you were trembling as if from a seizure. I cut the breeches from you, as the rain plastered it to your skin in a manner that made it difficult to simply pull from your body."

"Good heavens," she said horrified.

"However, your shirt and undergarments are drying by the grate."

"I have a strong constitution; you could have left me clothed," she said, unsure if she should be appalled or grateful at his impertinence.

"Do you?" His amused murmur washed over her.

A mass of hair that had been loosely pinned tumbled down her back; the icy water still soaking her strands wetted her neck and shoulders. Water trickled down her forehead, and she instinctively raised a hand to swipe it away. When cold air washed over the top of her breasts, she scrambled to draw the blanket to her throat.

A sharp indrawn breath from her rescuer had her fingers clenching reflexively on the blanket. Something heated, predatory, and dangerous swirled in the depths of his eyes, before his gaze hooded, and Payton was suddenly too petrified to move. Awareness of her vulnerability seeped into every crevice of her being. Despite the frigid night air, a bead of perspiration trickled down her spine, along with more rivulets from her hair. Payton would rather die than release the blanket to shift the heavy wetness from her neck. As circumspectly as possible, she catalogued every potential weapon in the small cottage: a poker iron, a carafe, a kettle, a china doll, and what looked like a broom.

Her heart clamored, but she held his gaze, afraid to look away lest he pounced. His unwavering stare prompted her into speech. "I am grateful for your assistance, and I thank you. Forgive my brusqueness, but it is not every day I wake undressed in a cottage alone with a stranger." *Good Lord.* It was his turn for his fingers to grip the armrest of his chair.

Maybe it was a terrible idea to remind him she was naked.

She attempted to smile. "I would be grateful if you would leave, so I may have some privacy." Thankfully her voice had not betrayed her nervousness.

Sudden laughter gleamed in his eyes. His gaze swept the tiny one room cottage, and then he looked at the door rattling under the power of rain and thunder raging outside. "No," he refuted with a low drawl, then inclined his head in mock politeness. "I fear we will both be denied the thing we want the most now."

His response jolted her, and her heart stuttered. She didn't need to wonder what he desired. His midnight gaze bore into her, a searchlight, as it caressed over her face. The very thought of him desiring her had a curious effect on Payton's senses. Slow, laden heat surged through her body, and it was not cold that had her nipples beading beneath the coverlet. The mash of fear and fascination made her feel ill.

Good Lord, what is wrong with me?

Never had she physically reacted so to a man, not even Lord Jensen, to whom she had been engaged. She'd only found Lord Jensen's embrace and kisses mildly enjoyable, but this man's bold stare was mystifyingly intriguing.

"You are being ungentlemanly, sir."

"I did not claim to be a gentleman. Though I will admit if the weather was different, I would grant you the privacy you seek." He waved to the door. "I will not prevent you from leaving if you wish." His words were a taunt, and she did not miss the way he straightened in the chair, as if anticipating her actions.

Payton wanted to toss her head and inform this man she would leave if he would not, but a wind howled, long and mournful, mocking her silent assertions. She searched for a clever and witty response, but could not find her tongue.

"Tell me, why were you traipsing about the stable at such an indecent hour dressed in that manner?"

"I do not have to explain my actions to you, sir, but I ride more comfortably without skirts hampering my movement. And *that* is all I sought this morning, the freedom to ride without judgment." Lest he saw her body's reaction and thought it was an invitation. It was certainly not.

"Hmm," he murmured noncommittally, steepling his long fingers on his muscular thighs.

Heat climbed her neck for noticing his virility. The flickering light from the fireplace illuminated the stark lines of his face and highlighted his strong jaw. He was unquestionably masculine and handsome, but also an unknown man who was staring at her with an expression she'd never encountered on another person. Payton's emotions vacillated between anger, apprehension, and intrigue. "You are staring, sir." *Please act more gentlemanly and avert your eyes.*

A smile curved his lips. "You are a beautiful woman."

"It is rude," she snapped, thoroughly rattled by his boldness and the unwilling interest stirring inside.

Provoking amusement lit his eyes. "Where I am from it is not rude to admire a ravishing jewel." His gaze lingered on her lips, before moving lower to her breasts, then down to her bare toes. He lifted his eyes to her face again. "And you are exquisite," he drawled.

Why had his words sounded so wicked? The silence seethed for endless seconds. To her utter mortification she felt her breasts getting heavy…achy; an unfamiliar but very pleasant sensation fluttered low in her abdomen. The air was thick with temptation, and disquiet simmered in Payton.

"Where are you from?" She pushed the words past her lips, desperately wanting to shatter the strange intimacy his words created.

Was it in her imagination that he stiffened?

He shifted in the chair, almost awkwardly. "Russia."

She nodded, at a loss for what to say. Never had she imagined she would have been caught in such an appalling situation. The one-room cottage was small but tastefully furnished. There was no apparent screen she could duck behind to dress. She did not care if her clothes were not dried. She would not remain exposed another second in his presence. "I need to get dressed."

"It is not wise. What you should be doing now is drying your tresses and keeping warm."

She knew the truth of his words. It was only a few weeks ago that she had recovered from a fever after being caught in a light drizzle on one of her long walks. Yet it was unthinkable to remain before this man in such a manner. All he would need to do is tug the blanket from her in one move. Was he a man capable of ravishing her even if she screamed no? Would she protest? *Bloody hell*. It was not like her to possess such raging unladylike musings, and she was mortified at the directions of her thoughts. They were wanton and served to remind her she was not a gentle bred English rose, more of a prickly American cactus.

As if he could feel her churning confusion he spoke, "I will not harm you, Lady—"

She took several deep breaths before speaking. "I am Miss Payton Peppiwell, Mr. Konstantinovich."

He inclined his head. "Thank you for the honor of your name. Despite the discomfort of this situation, I am pleased to make your acquaintance, Miss Peppiwell. What may I do to make you more comfortable?"

Wipe the desire from your eyes.

She glanced once more to the rattling door. It would be unfair to demand he leave.

Icy tendrils of water ran down her forehead into her eyes and onto her cheeks. Her hair needed to be dried, and she needed privacy. What a quandary. An embarrassing sneeze escaped her. "I—"

"Let me attend you. You will become ill if you clothe yourself in those sodden garments. Your hair needs to be dried, and I believe I can be of assistance."

She froze. *Good God.* He wanted to help her dry her hair? The impropriety of it was scandalous. Even without the decorum lessons she would have been appalled at his bald suggestion.

He stood, and she jumped to her feet. The air heated between them with a thrumming tension that had her throat tightening. The pounding rain was the only sound to pierce the disquieting silence. His eyes told Payton she was the most fascinating woman he'd ever beheld, and she was at a loss at how to respond to his unspoken seduction.

A shiver swept through her. His body appeared leanly muscled, hard, and graceful. She could also see the strength in his bearing. It took everything in her not to step back. Payton had never been more aware of the difference in strength and power between a man and a woman. For a few long seconds they glared at each other, and he tried a reassuring smile, but she narrowed her eyes in further warning.

"This situation is unexpected and obviously out of your

realm of experience, but I swear on my honor the doubts in your eyes are unwarranted. You have no need to fear me, Miss Peppiwell."

"I...I..." She hated being so flustered, and she really believed it was imperative to appear unflappable.

He arched a brow and cautiously reclaimed his seat where he studied her with calculating shrewdness. "Are you an intimate acquaintance of the duke and duchess?"

"Yes."

"And would you agree only another trustworthy friend would hold certain knowledge?"

She frowned. The duke and duchess were both highly unconventional and only called a few people friends. "Yes," she agreed.

His eyes bore into her for seconds, then he spoke, "The Duke of Calydon, Sebastian, and I have been friends for years. He met his duchess, Jocelyn, when she stormed his estate last year and held him at the point of a gun, a derringer to be precise."

A startled laugh squeezed from Payton's throat. She knew that story well. And as far as she was aware, only close intimate friends and family were acquainted with the scandalous manner in which Jocelyn had landed her duke.

He continued, "Her Grace gave birth to twins a couple months ago, and they are both dark haired and possess Sebastian's eyes. Lady Malory was first born by a mere two minutes, and Lord Julian was a pleasant surprise to the duke and duchess."

Who was he to hold such knowledge? Payton had been a guest at Sherring Cross a few times, and she had never encountered this man. But his revelations had the desired impact. Slow relief twisted through her, tension eased from her shoulders, and the defensive way she had been standing was relinquished. "You are friends with Sebastian and Jocelyn?"

"Sebastian and I have been close since childhood. I have only just met his duchess."

Payton thought of his words, carefully assessing him, realizing if he had wanted to attack her he could have taken her already. For all her bravado about knowing how to fight, he would have subdued her with little effort. Another sneeze rushed from her.

"Allow me to assist you in drying your hair." He pointed to a towel resting on a small burled walnut table.

His handsome face displayed no emotion, but there was an air of anticipation about him.

Everything about their encounter was already highly improper. She could set aside decorum this one time, and who would be privy to the knowledge that he assisted in drying her hair? Or that he had cut her trousers from her limbs. Hot color flooded her face, and she swallowed. "Thank you for your assistance. I am grateful. You must swear you will tell no one of what has occurred here."

Her capitulation had that strange light glinting in his eyes once more before he masked his expression.

"You have my word, Miss Peppiwell." He stood, graceful yet predatory, grabbed the towel, and stalked to her.

She met him in the middle of the room, breathing too heavily for comfort. Slipping past him, a death grip on the voluminous blanket, Payton sat in the chair closest to the fire.

Oh God, what am I doing?

Chapter Three

Miss Payton Peppiwell wore sensuality like a second skin, unstudied and wholly natural. She was the most exquisite young lady Mikhail had ever seen. She was neither tall nor short, just about the right height to fit perfectly into the curves of his shoulders. Her voice was rich and smoky, laced with carnality and wickedness. She had deep auburn hair, brown eyes so fathomless they would appear black, if not for the flashes of dark gold at their center, a delicate nose, and elegant cheekbones. Her honeyed skin was unblemished and radiant, and even swaddled in blankets, her curves were so richly pronounced his mouth dried. When he'd cut away the wet clothes, he had barely spared a glance at her naked body, too concerned with stopping the terrible shivers that had been shaking her form, but now all he could do was stare like an untried youth.

Why was she at Sherring Cross? Certainly she was not a lady of the *haute monde*. Her hauteur would have been more evident, and she would have selfishly persisted in demanding he left the cabin, despite the inclement weather.

A shudder went through her as he started to dry her hair. He glanced down and suppressed a smile. She had the blanket clutched almost to her chin. A brutal fist of lust had slammed into his gut when he'd caught a tantalizing glimpse of her breasts earlier. Though she was skittish, the dark gold of her eyes glittered with interest and sensual awareness.

With the right seductive touch, her ripe curves could be his for the taking. He could coax her into parting her thighs, then bury his aching length to the hilt. The knowledge settled in Mikhail's groin, hardening his cock into painful need, disturbing him with the strength of his response. It had been years since a woman had the ability to rouse him without him mentally allowing it. Anger at his lack of temperance over his passion twisted through his veins.

What the hell is wrong with me...concentrate. He buried the flare of unease. It would not do to unsettle her further with the dark edge trying to wind itself into his heart.

He did his best to dry her hair without tangling it, trying not to linger over its softness and beauty. Her hair was thick and gloriously abundant. An image of how she had looked seated atop his horse rushed through him. He could picture the curtain of her hair shimmering around them in cascading waves as she rode *him*, trembling on his cock from the pleasure he would give her.

Arrgh, cease!

Mikhail tried to subdue his lurid thoughts. Probably he needed to step outside into the squall and endure the frigid rain to clear his head. Miss Peppiwell's hair jerked from his grasp as she glanced at him quickly, then away to gaze into the fire. More than once she'd shifted to peek up at him while clutching the blanket to her throat, her exquisite heart-shaped face filled with desire...and uncertainty.

The aroma of berries wafted on a gentle breeze to his nose, and he prevented himself from inhaling her scent further. She was already afraid of him. Her eyes flicked across the room in a quick assessment, and he noted her lingering gaze on the iron poker by the roaring fire. She heard his low chuckle, for she looked back to him, a cool expression hiding the fear she had flinched with earlier.

She was no wilting miss. He saw the defiant courage and was impressed. Many young ladies would have been beyond hysteria by now, liberally indulging in swooning fits and the vapors, considering he was not successfully hiding the lust slicing at his self-control.

The silence lingering between them, as he lifted the heavy mass of her hair to blot the final wetness from it, was tense. How could he put her at ease? First he had to rein in the blasted hunger twisting in his gut. He had more control of his passions than he was currently displaying.

She sneezed into the blanket, three times in quick succession.

There was no kitchen or parlor or a hearth for cooking. He vaguely remembered playing games in his youth here with Sebastian and Anthony when they had wanted to escape the main house. "We may have stumbled upon the cottage in which the Calydon children played."

"I think you are right."

Though she sounded relieved he had started a discourse, she was ramrod stiff in the chair.

"Your hair will not fully dry, however, most of the wetness is dealt with. I'm regretful to say I see no teapot or any liquor to help you with the chill."

She graced him with a wobbly smile. "We will simply make do with our sparse accommodations. It was fortuitous you found the cottage when it was needed. The horse I rode, he is your stallion?"

He hesitated. "Yes, I trained him as a gift to Calydon."

"He is a magnificent animal. I pray he will return safely

to the stables."

"Sage will be fine," Mikhail reassured. "He is well trained."

"That is what you do, train horses?"

"In a manner of speaking."

Her gaze narrowed. It was hard to not miss the intelligence and curiosity lurking in her gaze. "You train horses, or you do not, there is no 'in a manner of' about it."

"It is one of the things I do." Mikhail was careful to keep the amusement from his tone. He could imagine what it would be like if he revealed himself to be a prince. Miss Peppiwell would probably start to scream, if only to bring attention to their location to ensure she entrapped him for marriage. Not that he was foolishly tempted to reveal his identity.

He'd sought his cousin's estate to get away from the oppressive weight of society's expectations, and the fact that he would soon be immersing himself in England's *haute monde*, a place he had not entered since Madam Anya's perfidy. He'd had enough vile rumors to deflect in his own homeland and had shunned the *haute monde* whenever he visited England, but now Mikhail had little choice. Everyone was expecting to meet the new Duke of Avondale.

They would simply have to wait. He'd lived with depraved scandal for years and had just escaped another. The realization that, if he were not careful now, Mikhail could land himself back in the dark mire of vicious rumors and unending ignominy, set his teeth on edge.

Hell. It had been an unpleasant shock to find Sherring Cross bursting at the seams with the very guests he had wanted to avoid until it became absolutely necessary. Lady Calydon was hosting a small, intimate house party, which unfortunately coincided with Mikhail's arrival. He craved a few months of peace without the trappings of society, and he was not about to compromise it because of Miss Peppiwell's unease, but he would do everything possible to make her relax.

A sigh escaped her, drawing his attention to her lovely face.

"And what else do you do?"

"I sometimes advise others on estate matters," he answered vaguely.

A quick frown flashed across her face. "I see. Like a financial advisor?"

"Yes."

She pushed strands of wet hair off her cheeks. "And you provide this service for the Duke of Calydon?" Her shoulders had relaxed a bit, but her eyes still glowed with wariness.

"I have advised him on several estate and financial matters over the years."

Her direct stare was unwavering. "And you also do this for other lords?"

Mikhail thought of his father, brothers, and other cousins. Even the recently crowned Tsarevich Alexander had solicited Mikhail's expertise because of his acumen with money.

"Yes."

"And were you invited to Lady Calydon's house party?" Miss Peppiwell's voice trembled, but her eyes were challenging.

"No, my presence at Sherring Cross is a happy coincidence." He doubted he hid the inflection of sarcasm from his tone, but she nodded, seeming satisfied.

"I promise you no harm, Miss Peppiwell." Mikhail kept his voice low and crooning, as if speaking to one of his horses. "As soon as the rain lessens, I will ensure you are returned to the main house discreetly before the guests rise."

It would not bode well if those in attendance realized he and Miss Peppiwell had been alone for any duration.

Her eyes sparkled with rancor. "I have learned all too well the perfidy of promises; I have no faith in them."

Ah. Already jaded. For one so young, it was a pity. "You can have faith in mine."

A subtle tremor flowed through her limbs, and incredulity flashed in her eyes. "I think not," she all but growled, then ruined her ferocity by sneezing.

His fingers brushed against the exposed skin at her nape, and she flinched. Their conversation was not relaxing her at all. The awareness of how worried she must be killed all his longings of lust, attacking his resistance mercilessly. "You have no need to fear my presence, Miss Peppiwell."

She gave him an assessing glance, then lifted her chin a notch. "I am not afraid."

So her method was not to admit fear lest he saw it as a weakness. His admiration rose. He strolled to the fireplace and collected the poker. She watched him with a frown that broke into a cautious smile when he handed it to her.

"I see," she said, her eyes now dancing with humor. "This is you giving me permission to defend myself, if you should do anything untoward?"

The transformation to her features when she relaxed was astonishing. Mikhail was used to beauty, but Miss Peppiwell's unique charms had a delightful effect on his senses. The young lady also seemed unaware of her own desirability. There was no predatory calculation in her eyes, no smoldering glances from beneath lowered lashes. Was that because she was not aware of his wealth and stature? If he were to reveal himself, would she change? The thought left him cold. "Yes, I am granting you permission if you feel threatened in any manner."

Her lips twitched. "You are brave indeed, sir. I may think your provoking stares are untoward," she said teasingly.

It had been more than a decade since he had felt such an interest in a woman. But then, it had been years since any lady had looked at him without avarice glittering in her eyes.

Belonging to one of the most prominent families in Russia was not as fortuitous as it seemed. He liked being able to pretend normality with her. It gave him freedom to speak and act in a manner in which he ordinarily would not allow.

"Allow me to make amends for the unintentional impropriety of my actions. Will you picnic with me later today, if the rain stops?"

"You want to take me on a picnic?" She queried with undisguised bemusement.

Mikhail himself was startled when the words escaped his lips. He should be doing anything to place distance between himself and this enticing female. His one true purpose should be to hide his identity, not compromise it by wooing a woman. It would not do for the scandal he left at home to follow him to London. She was destroying his common sense. "Yes."

"Why?"

"Your charm has delighted me, and I wish to spend more time in your company." What the hell was he saying?

She appeared nonplussed, before her enticing lips stretched into a wide smile. An irrepressible dimple appeared, and he wanted to kiss it. Mikhail almost snorted at his fanciful thoughts.

"I would enjoy a picnic, but my parents will object to you calling on me." A quick frown settled on her face. "I…please ignore what I said. I would be delighted."

He nodded, a curious feeling shifting inside him. He had not expected her to agree to his impulsive invitation. He tried to assess the need that had prodded him to ask her and was frustratingly blank. This was so unlike him, tension wove its way into his gut.

"Please turn and go to the far corner. I need to make myself presentable."

After wrapping her hair in the second towel, he walked to the wall farthest from her and closed his eyes. Sounds shuffled in the cottage, and it was a testament to his needs that he could make out the distinct noise over the pounding rain. He bit back a groan when he heard the blanket slither to the ground. More rustles, and then a soft gasp from her, no doubt the shock of the wet clothes on her skin.

"You can turn around."

Mikhail braced himself, and then faced her. She was the most ludicrous sight he had ever beheld, with the towel perched haphazardly on her head, a mass of tendrils rioting around her face, her shirt limp with dampness, and the blanket wrapped around her body at least three times to make a bulky toga. And yet she was the most refreshing woman he had ever laid eyes on, with her flashing defiant eyes and lopsided smile.

Damnable nonsense to be so captivated by a female he knew nothing about. He was fully aware of the blackened and treacherous thoughts a bewitching face can hide. Perhaps it was incidental that she affected him so strongly. After all, it had been several months since he'd bedded a woman.

"What do we do now?" she asked with a nervous chuckle, her eyes flickering to the narrow cot and then back to him.

Christ.

She was aware of the lust simmering between them, but from the dazed confusion in her eyes, Mikhail could tell she had never been exposed to passion. The knowledge should have urged caution, but it only captivated him further. *She ought to have a buck tooth and be prone to vapors*, he thought in pure disgruntlement, not trusting his fascination. Maybe then he would be able to resist her lures.

"There is a card pack on the mantel and a second blanket on the bed. It is best you remain close by the fire to keep warm and dry your clothing. May I interest you in a game of *Gusarik*?"

She repeated the word slowly, rolling it around on her tongue with her delightful accent. After a quick look toward the door still shaking under the storm, she graced him with a small smile of acquiescence. "I have never played, but I would learn to pass the time."

"I will happily educate you in the arts of *Gusarik*."

"I am a quick study."

Her eyes sparkled, and he wondered if she was aware of the heated invitation glowing in them. Against his own inclination, he stepped closer, and her eyes flared wide in alarm and undisguised intrigue. *Do not do it*, the saner part of him growled. He dipped his head, and she swallowed, but she did not retreat.

For God's sake, save yourself, Miss Peppiwell.

Their mouths only scant inches apart, she wetted her lips. It was a nervous reaction to his nearness, but everything in him narrowed on her lips. He was starving for a taste of something new, something sweet and innocent, without the sly memory of depravity distorting its purity. He inhaled, then shuddered, so potent was her scent. *This is madness.*

"Is this where I reach for the poker and bash you?" she asked huskily.

He snapped his gaze to hers, and the wicked amusement dancing in her honey eyes pushed a soft laugh from Mikhail. "No, *milaya moya*."

Relief and disappointment flashed across her face. "What does *milaya moya* mean?"

He hesitated. The endearment had slipped from him without thought. He was losing control too fast…too suddenly.

"It must mean something dreadful if you do not wish to divulge," she teased.

Cold caution settled in his gut. "My sweet…it means my sweet."

Beguiling color dusted her skin. "Please refer to me as Miss Peppiwell, Mr. Konstantinovich. We are not intimates and 'my sweet'…is outrageous and inappropriate," she said with a glare that lessened the twinkle in her eyes.

She was irresistibly fascinating.

"You will call me Mikhail, and I will refer to you as Payton." He waved to encompass the small cottage. "I feel our situation is intimate enough for us to dispel with pretentious formalities."

She pursed her lips, considering him. "You sound like a man used to giving commands...Mikhail."

"And you sound like an utterly delightful and challenging woman, Payton." *A challenge which I accept...mayhap to my detriment.*

Bald interest glowed in her eyes. "So should I release the poker?"

It was then he noted her fingers were curled over the iron in a firm grip.

His lips twitched, but he suppressed the smile. "Do you feel threatened?"

"Most assuredly."

Yet he saw no anxiety in her. In fact, her gaze dipped to his mouth, and his bloody heart lurched. "Do you fear I will kiss you?"

"No...I fear I would encourage you." She sucked in an audible breath and lifted shocked eyes to his at her uncensored response.

"I...I..."

"Please do not apologize. I admire your honesty."

"You mean my unladylike utterances."

"I welcome any wicked words to spill from your lips." Never had he spoken so to a lady, but it was as if their unusual situation gave him freedom to act without fear of judgment or entrapment. And it was more than evident to him, her enticing boldness was unnatural.

The space between them heated, and his control wavered. Scowling at his undisciplined reaction, he stepped away from her tempting warmth, and a soft exhalation of relief puffed from her.

Mikhail felt the weight of her gaze on him as he added a log to the fire. He wasted no time seeing to their comforts before the hearth. She settled on the blanket facing him, and he did his best to appear nonchalant. For certainly she would run from the cottage and brave the storm if she understood the ruthless will he was exerting on himself, still trying to determine if, before the dawn crested, he would pleasure her with his fingers, then his tongue and cock, breaking the rigid chain of control he had exercised over his passions for ten long years.

In all his life Mikhail had never been so tempted by beauty.

Tested by a smile.

Beguiled by a scent.

Enchanted by nervous laughter.

He didn't appreciate his visceral reaction to her; in truth it made him wary that someone was capable of making the walls he had so ruthlessly built tremble, but he felt helpless to stop the cravings erupting inside him. If he had believed in such nonsense, Mikhail would have thought the desperate clenching sensation roaring to life inside was him falling into love.

An utterly implausible state he had no desire to suffer, considering he would never be able to allow one of the most crucial, intrinsic, and necessary desires between lovers.

Mutual touch.

Chapter Four

"You wish to remain secreted from society for several weeks?"

Prince Alexander Mikhail Konstantinovich, the Count of Montgomery and the Duke of Avondale—Mikhail to his close friends and family—stared at the surprised and irritated face of his most trustworthy confidant and cousin, Sebastian Thornton, the Duke of Calydon. It was not a common occurrence for Mikhail to surprise his normally unflappable cousin. Far from it. But the expressions that raced across the man's face suggested Mikhail had said he wished to visit a brothel—a place Mikhail had an acute distaste for. "Yes."

"Why?"

Tension stole through Mikhail. "You know the reasons."

His cousin was aware of Mikhail's aversion to scandal and the whispers that could sneak behind the rigid armor he'd built around his life and pierce him when he least expected.

Calydon grunted. "You walked away from Princess Tatiana in a crowded ballroom with her clinging to your sleeves and crying. Heartless, cold, a miscreant, vile seducer of innocence, debauched rake are a few of the words Aunt Josephine told me you were called. The princess is shamelessly insisting you compromised her, and her family is expecting a wedding." Calydon scrubbed a hand over his face, anger snapping in his eyes. "You are the Duke of Avondale, whom all of London is so blasted eager to meet. When you asked me yesterday not to introduce you, I thought you meant for a day or two, not weeks," he ended on a near growl.

Mikhail remained silent.

"And what of your ambitions to find a wife? The mammas of the marriage mart will happily throw balls and parties in your honor, and the leading belles of the *haute monde* will present themselves."

Mikhail arched a brow. "I have no such ambition; it is father's hope." A humorless chuckle rolled through him. "In time I will marry. I know my duty to my lands and titles."

Though I may have very well found a woman I could marry. He stiffened, a jerk of shock punching him at his unbidden thought. It seemed Payton Peppiwell was firmly lodged in his subconscious. Never was it more apparent he could not blame the prick in his iron control on the two shots of vodka and three glasses of brandy he'd indulged.

Calydon leaned forward, planting his elbows on his desk. "And what of Princess Tatiana? Your father's health will not stand up to you not repairing the damage in your relationship. You know he has long dreamed of an alliance between the Konstantinoviches and the Kraznovses."

Mikhail's father had a heart condition, and he used it to try and manipulate Mikhail shamelessly. While he normally indulged his father, he would not marry a woman simply because the *Dvoryanstvo* demanded it. "She is ruined by her own actions. She has claimed I seduced her when she knows it is not so. Father loves Princess Tatiana as he would his own daughter. Her brother, Prince Kirill, is one of my closest friends, but I will not be pressured into marriage because she tried to force my hand. She is insisting she is *enceinte* with my child, but I never touched her. I suspect she may very well be, but the culprit is without wealth and would be unsuitable."

The desperate, tear-filled face of Princess Tatiana floated through his mind. "My father wanted our union because he desires to see me with a wife and children. But when I do take such a step, it will be because *I* decide it," Mikhail said flatly.

Calydon grimaced. "I know all too well how difficult it is to accept the betrayal of someone for whom you held affections. Princess Tatiana is a family friend. I urge you to not let her foolish actions embitter you."

Mikhail stilled. He was already hardened; he doubted there was room for any other emotions to worm their way into his heart.

Have your forgotten this morning so soon? His conscience prodded. The memory of laughing dark eyes surfaced. There was a void in his soul, and he swore that for the first time in years, while bantering with Payton, he had felt a bit of peace. The notion was absolutely ludicrous…and frightfully intriguing.

"I was simply a monetary means to an end for Tatiana. I doubt I will make acquaintance with a young lady who can see beyond the power of money and connections."

Calydon's brow arched. "There are many young ladies who desire marriage for other reasons."

"It is neither here nor there." Mikhail was not sure if there had ever been a time in history when marriage matches were not about money or political alliances. All his life he had been pursued for wealth and prestige, and he would admit the idea of a woman looking at him without avarice glowing in her eyes was pleasant.

Like Payton.

Seeking a distraction from his viscerally disturbing thoughts, Mikhail looked out into the gardens. The duchess strolled by, arm in arm with her younger sister, Lady Victoria.

Their heads were dipped close, their lovely faces animated. Mikhail remembered a time when his cousin had been deeply jaded and had sworn never to marry or trust a woman. Now Sebastian had a duchess and children. The sudden ache filling Mikhail's chest was unexpected and curious, but not altogether uncomfortable. "I never thought you would allow yourself to trust a woman."

A smile creased the duke's face, drawing attention to the rapier scar on his left cheek. His eyes darkened, and the love in them actually caused a slow, uncomfortable jerk of Mikhail's heart.

"The right woman can be trusted with everything that you are—the darkness and the light," Sebastian answered, his eyes flicking to the gardens, seeking his duchess. At that moment she and Lady Victoria threw back their heads and laughed without an ounce of decorum. The duchess chortled, and it warmed Mikhail to see Sebastian's reaction to her delight. The duke had been cold for far too long, and Mikhail was damned glad for his cousin's good fortune.

"I am glad you found her," Mikhail said softly.

"And I would be doubly glad if you would find a similar happiness."

Mikhail contained his flinch. "I am content."

"No…you merely exist, closing yourself from life because you fear hurting. I know, for I did the same for years until I met my duchess."

Rage lit in his veins, and he met Sebastian's eyes. "You compare our pasts?" Mikhail asked, the raw edge of dark emotions tugging at his calm facade.

The duke's eyes hooded, and he sank into his chair. "Never," he said. "I cannot comprehend your pain, but I can identify with the haunting distance I see in your eyes. It is a lonely path to eschew female companionship. I think it is a similar thought your father had and why he pushed you to consider Princess Tatiana."

Mikhail had no want for the affections his cousin spoke about. For ten long years he'd exercised the utmost control over his body and emotions, forming liaisons on his terms. Whenever he lusted, he slaked it with minimal fuss by women who understood he offered nothing and accepted the way he made love—with his lover positioned on hands and knees, ensuring minimal skin contact.

"Have you directed the housekeeper to place me in the west wing, away from all the guests?" Mikhail asked, directing the conversation to where he wanted. It was the reason he had chosen to bed down in the stable's loft last evening. The chamber that had been readied for him was on the same floor as the other guests. He'd requested the change and then had spent hours riding, even going as far as to dine in the village's inn closest to Sherring Cross.

Calydon lifted a brow at his diversion. He nodded and then brought them solidly back to business. "Mother and Jocelyn have a full itinerary to welcome you into society in a few weeks."

Mikhail grimaced. "No," he growled.

Calydon set aside his correspondence, directing his undivided attention to Mikhail. "You have your seat to claim in Parliament. There are connections to be fostered. While it is appealing to bury your head in the country, you cannot ignore the duties to your title for months."

"They will wait," Mikhail said flatly. The memory of gazes burning with rabid speculations and whispers of *whore* and *brothel* sliced through him. The scandal of his life would *never* be over, and it would follow him wherever he traveled, but he would control when it haunted his steps. The minute he was introduced to society, the vultures would seek his past as if it were carrion, simply because that is what they do. Then the gossip would ride the air and somehow find itself into every drawing room in London. Despite the vileness of the rumors, matchmaking mothers and young ladies would plot his downfall with avaricious glee, throw themselves at his feet, sneak into his bed, and pretend to be pregnant by him...

He snapped his teeth together in annoyance. He would delay his introduction for as long as possible. Another scandal had urged him to leave his home, family, and country, to assume a mantle in which he had never been interested. All his life, his heart had belonged to Russia. After one of his cousins had died without issue six months ago, knowledge of the responsibilities he would have to assume in England had settled in Mikhail's gut like a heavy boulder. But it had been easy to give in to his mother's gentle persuasion to visit Sherring Cross, for it came when he had wanted to leave Tatiana's pleadings and her tear-stained face, and the scandal her betrayal and his subsequent reaction to it had wrought, behind.

A heavy sigh slipped from Calydon. "The ball my mother has planned in your honor is a mere six weeks away. I will advise Jocelyn and the household they are not to refer to you by your titles until it is necessary. Mother will be sorely disappointed."

Mikhail had known his aunt by marriage would turn her matchmaking eyes his way. She'd already written to him when she learned he would claim his duchy with a reminder he must be in *need* of a wife. From Russia he'd heard the meddlesome wheels turning in Lady Radcliffe's head. "I urge you to advise your mother to reconsider the ball in its entirety. I have no need for an introduction to England's *haute monde*. When I am ready I will simply appear."

Calydon chuckled. "Even so secluded at Sherring Cross, whispers of the chatter in London have reached our ears. All are awaiting the arrival of the new duke, especially the *maters*. My mother thinks it is somewhat of a coup, to host the first ball you'll attend in society. Nothing I say will deter her."

Mikhail grunted and pushed to his feet. He moved to

the windows facing the rolling grounds of the estate. Several guests strolled on the lawns, and some were playing archery. His gaze searched, feeding the need in him to find Payton once more. He was decidedly curious to see if she had the same effect on him without the intimacy of their enclosure and the possibilities of seduction on the air. He doubted it… but he still wanted—no, needed—to know.

"You look for someone?"

"Yes."

Calydon's eyes sharpened with interest. "A woman?"

The blasted man's tone was too hopeful. Mikhail briefly debated not answering. "A Miss Payton Peppiwell," he said, trying to sound casual. He feared he failed, from the pleased smile that creased Sebastian's lips.

"The young lady and her family only arrived at Sherring Cross late yesterday evening. How is it you have come to make Miss Peppiwell's acquaintance when it is barely dawn?"

He grunted noncommittally and Sebastian laughed, then sobered at whatever he saw in Mikhail's face.

"Is she still chaste?" Sebastian demanded with a narrow-eyed glare.

"What is it to you?"

"It obviously escaped your notice—she is family."

Peppiwell. Mikhail's other cousin, Lord Anthony's wife's surname had been Peppiwell. "I do not go around seducing women. The squall forced our early meeting, and we were together in the cottage you and I played in as children for a while. I returned her discreetly."

Sebastian's shoulders visibly relaxed, and then he frowned. "Payton doesn't know who you are?"

"No. She'd demanded to know if I worked for you, so I gave her vague responses. They were not lies, but nor were they a full disclosure in what capacity I advised you, or trained horses for you."

"Did she interest you?" Curiosity was rife in his cousin's tone.

Memory of the artless hunger in her gaze and tentative smile swam across Mikhail's vision, and he had to grit his teeth against the arousal curling through him. "Maybe."

He could feel the shock pouring from his cousin, and Mikhail understood. It had been years since he admitted interest in a woman.

"You do not sound pleased."

He met Sebastian's gaze. "She is the only woman to challenge my discipline in years." Mikhail had spent years distancing himself from the women of the Russian court, content to live with the coldness encasing his heart. Now this slip of a girl threatened his resolve. Was it even prudent to think about a woman who made those walls quaver? He could not allow anything to reduce him again to the pitiful boy he'd been after surviving Madam Anya's depravity. He closed his eyes, drawing upon his iron control, forcing all pain and regret into abeyance.

He should relinquish all thoughts of Payton Peppiwell.

A thoughtful frown settled on the duke's face. "Are you saying you have a different reaction to her than with other women?"

"Yes."

Calydon slowly rose and moved to stand beside him. "Do you intend to pursue her?"

Mikhail's mind muddled. *No.* She had only been a dangerous anomaly, albeit intriguing. He grunted, unable to give voice to the dual need warring inside.

"Mikhail," Sebastian said softly, a note of apology in his tone.

Mikhail braced himself against the last thing he wanted to speak. *Do not mention Madam Anya.*

Sebastian hesitated as if sensing his turmoil. "If you do decide to explore the interest she stirred, be kind to her."

Mikhail clenched his jaw. He knew his cousin wanted to

say more, and he appreciated the restraint. "If I did, I would not treat her unkindly."

"Not intentionally. But we both know you will hold back a part of yourself with Payton at all times. She deserves so much more."

Why were they even having this pointless discourse? "I would not waste my time with a pursuit. That would require me revealing my status, and I welcome solitude too much now to think of courtship."

But what if you could endure a normal relationship?

It was as if the devil himself slinked from the bowels of hell and whispered the thought in his ear. Mikhail was almost certain he could touch the spot beneath his ear and feel temptation's cold kiss.

Blasted hell.

What in God's name was a normal relationship? Since his kidnapping, and sexual torture at the hands of one of Russia's most infamous courtesans, Mikhail abhorred touch. Even when he eventually took a wife, he faced the risk of having her turn to another man for affections he could not give.

Christ. He had already experienced it with a woman he'd thought he loved. Lady Olga. He'd always recoiled from the icy pain of her grasping touch, and she'd sought another.

So why was he even thinking of taking Payton on a picnic?

The mere thought of pursuing her had emotions he'd not felt in years twisting in his gut—anxiety, dread, and electrifying excitement. He preferred to dwell in the cold void where no pain or memory of humiliation resided. But what if learning her allowed him something he'd thought he would never reclaim—the sensual glide of a lover's touch, the press of her lips against his throat, the fan of her breath as she trailed hot kisses down to his stomach and enveloped his cock in her sublime heat, a simple hug when he was weary?

Mikhail had never suffered such a quandary.

Chapter Five

Proper young ladies did not imagine being kissed senseless, of being ravished and held in an illicit embrace by unknown gentlemen. Never had it been more evident that Payton was not proper, nor a well-bred young lady, like those who peppered the *haute monde*. She had fantasized about how Mikhail's hands would feel against her bare skin, dreamed of his lips pressed softly to hers, of waltzing with him under the stars. Of what it would have been like if he had taken her in his arms and kissed her. Gently marauding or savagely ravishing?

Dear heavens.

Payton dried her hair fully and changed into a soft blue day dress, but it seemed she had not escaped a cold and fever as she had hoped. It was the only explanation for the burning curiosity that had lighted in her veins as they had played cards by the fire and now continued to torment her hours later.

The whole encounter had been so surreal, so appealing. Since living in England, this had been the first time she had gotten a glimpse of what life with an ordinary man could be like. A small cottage…well mayhap not so small, but the quiet intimacy while they lazed by the fire, talking, reading, playing chess or cards with not a care in the world.

Blast the man. He made her question the resolve to guard her heart so stringently, and he was untitled. Her family would have a fit if they could peek at Payton's intimate thoughts, and she finally admitted she must do something about their incessant badgering her to marry. She craved something else, not a life of adventure or wealth, but one filled with calm acceptance of her abilities and passion. She had never imagined it would be so daunting to inform her mother and aunt she desired simply to marry a man of her choosing.

Lifting the pen from the inkwell, she wrote to her sister Phillipa. Payton felt as if their relationship had been strained since Lord Jensen jilted her, but Phillipa insisted it was not so. Payton knew better. Hurting, she had thoughtlessly blamed her sister for Lord Jensen's coolness, when he was the one who had been lacking. They had since repaired their relationship, but Payton had not unwound to confide in her sister the way she had done in the past. Her embarrassment and hurt had been too profound.

Payton hoped sharing with her sister now would reaffirm the closeness they'd once had. And she also desperately wanted the counsel of someone who did not live for high society. She snatched a piece of foolscap paper from the desk drawer, placed it on the small walnut desk where she settled, and started to write.

> *Dearest Phillipa,*
>
> *I have missed you so, sister. It has been a few weeks since we last exchanged letters. How are you and Lord Anthony? I tried to escape Mother and Aunt Florence to visit you in Baybrook, but I fear they would only follow me and ruin the idyllic and blissful time you must be enjoying with Anthony.*

I have met someone

I confess I write to you now because I am in desperate need of your guidance. I met someone this morning on an early morning ride; a Mr. Mikhail Konstantinovich. The inclement weather forced us to share a cottage together, alone, for a few hours. I have never met a man so alarmingly handsome and fascinating. Though he acted gentlemanly, for the most part, the force of his presence was felt in a manner I have never encountered before. From a mere stare, my heart raced, and I ached with the need for him to press his lips to mine.

There, I have immortalized my scandalous thoughts. He has crumbled the disinterest I had formed in courtship. He is a mister, a man of affairs of sorts to Calydon, so mother and father would never approve of me walking with him, yet I desire to. The knowledge he would have no expectation of strict behavior and this ridiculous notion of ladylike propriety from me, is so refreshing and tempting. He invited me to a picnic, and I eagerly consented. Now I doubt my actions. What would be the purpose of walking with someone our parents would never approve of? I will also admit the knowledge that I will turn twenty-one in several months has been hovering. If I were to really form an attachment with Mr. Konstantinovich I could eventually marry him without Father's consent. I would hate to disappoint them so, and I may be getting ahead of myself. In fact, mayhap it was our unusual situation that has led me to believe he is charming.

Though I find him interesting, there is also a deeper dread slowly rearing its head. What if beneath the surface of his handsomeness he is just

*as callous and unfeeling as Lord Jensen? I had
thought I would have only been leery of someone
belonging to the* haute monde, *however, it seems
men in general have gained my mistrust.*

I fear I am rambling.

*On to other news. I have started a new story
which I hope to gift to the twins. I am quite aware
they will not be able to read it, so please quit rolling
your eyes. But when they are older, they will know
this wonderful story, of a brother and sister flying
on dragons to save the kingdom of Gruyn, was
written for them.*

*I wish you and Lord Anthony would visit
Sherring Cross. You are missing the twins' rapid
growth, and our dear sister Phoebe is blossoming
too fast. She turns sixteen in a few weeks and she
eagerly speaks of having a season. She needs your
guidance as well, for we know how treacherous
those waters can be. If I do not see you in the next
couple of weeks, I will resolve to steal away for a
visit without Mama and Aunt Florence.*

Your sister, Payton

With efficient motions she folded the paper, sealed it in an
envelope, and scrawled directions for it to be delivered
to her sister's country home. Rushing from her chamber,
Payton descended the winding staircase to the lower floors.
Thankfully, it was early enough that the halls were empty of
guests. Leaving the letter on the mantel, she turned in the
direction of the parlor.

She would walk with Mikhail in the afternoon. She tried
to rein in the wash of anticipation. The sensations he'd made
her feel were unlike any Payton had ever known. And the
blasted man had not even stolen a kiss. Lord Jensen had

kissed her several times, and she had never felt feverish.

Nearing the parlor, she faltered. She'd had a thought about Lord Jensen that had not left her heart clenching in discomfort. But it did direct her attention to the matter at hand and away from a tempting blue-eyed devil. She had not been able to enter her chamber earlier without being seen.

Aunt Florence had been waiting in Payton's chamber with a list of all eligible gentlemen present at Sherring Cross. The paper held each man's name, their respective title, and an estimation of their annual income. Shock and distaste had filled Payton, and her objection to the list had been smothered by her aunt's distress at seeing Payton bedraggled and swaddled in a blanket. It had been hellacious reassuring her aunt nothing had happened. It had been tempting to speak a lie, and say she had been in the cottage alone, but she'd not wanted to risk the truth coming out somehow.

She was now walking to meet her mother as if she were heading to the guillotine. Maybe she should have bent the truth. Upon reaching the parlor, she gripped the doorknob, straightened her shoulders, and took a deep breath. Soft footsteps sounded in the foyer, and she lifted her eyes in their direction.

Mikhail.

His gaze flicked over her in a quick assessment, and she swore his blue eyes darkened. Yet he did not slow his stride or acknowledge her, except for a slow quirk of his lips and a wink. Startling delight suffused her, and for some reason it felt natural to return a slow wink. An acknowledgment of their scandalous encounter.

Then an expression of utter shock settled on his face. Was it because he winked, or because she responded in kind?

A gentle clearing of throat tore her gaze away from him, to see the duke.

Where did he come from?

Heat crawled up her neck. Obviously they had been discussing business matters in the duke's office. She needed to acclimatize herself to the idea of Mikhail's presence in the main house, considering he was one of the duke's men of affairs. Sebastian's impenetrable gaze shifted between her and Mikhail before he greeted her.

"Your Grace," she murmured with a quick smile, then wrenched the door open, escaping into the parlor.

Not that it was much of an escape. Twin turquoise eyes swung in her direction. If Payton had not known better, she would have thought someone had died. The room seethed with disquiet. Her mother, Mrs. Katherine Peppiwell, and her Aunt Florence, the Countess of Merryweather, bore a similar appalled countenance.

"You were trapped in a cabin with a commoner. This must *never* come out," her mother snapped.

There were absolutely no polite preliminaries or even the chance to seat herself before the start of the attack. The sharp retort hovering on Payton's lips died. *Oh, Mama.*

When would this desire to marry her to a lord end? Father had made several connections with prominent families since their sojourn to England, taking the Peppiwell family closer to the heart of the social elevation they desired. Before her sister Phillipa's marriage to Lord Anthony, it had not been so. But Lord Anthony was referred to as a lion of commerce with a golden touch for investments, and her father was more than thrilled with their connection. It infuriated Payton that her family still insisted she needed to wed, and to a titled man.

"Did you hear me, young lady?" her mother demanded fiercely.

Payton almost rolled her eyes, but caught herself in the nick of time. Another lecture on propriety would not be welcome. "Yes, Mother."

"My nerves are still unsettled to know you were alone

with a commoner," her aunt fretted.

Exasperation rushed through Payton and she sauntered over to sit in front of the table by the window. "*I* am a commoner, Aunt. And as secluded as Sherring Cross is, I fail to see how society would discover my unintentional faux pas. Mr. Konstantinovich did rescue me from being seriously injured and acted as a true gentleman in assisting my return to the main house without being seen."

"Did he touch you or act inappropriately in any manner?" her mother demanded with narrowed eyes.

"Of course not! He is a respectable acquaintance of His Grace." Her mind flitted to the caress against her lips, and the potent desire on his face when he had inhaled her scent. For a heart-stopping moment, she had thought he would truly kiss her. And Payton had been unsure of what her reaction would have been. She was grateful he had pulled away and released her from the mesmerizing effect of his dark sensuality.

Aunt Florence sighed. "We have been most fortunate to receive an invitation to the duchess's intimate house party. There will be many suitable *titled* gentlemen in attendance, who are closely acquainted with such a wonderful family. The season is drawing to a close, my dear, and you need to snag a gentleman before they all retire to the country for hunting. It would not do for you to be presented for a third season."

Payton had not been presented anywhere. Her entry into society had been unremarkable, and she was only remembered as *the jilted*. Not as someone to whom a promise had been broken, but as *the jilted,* as if such a sobriquet defined her. While she was happy to be a part of the select few the Duchess of Calydon called "friend", Payton still found mixing with lords and ladies unpleasant. She'd resolved to spend the next two weeks soaking up Sebastian and Jocelyn's kindness and hospitality, but Payton was more interested in visiting the twins and reading them stories they were too young to understand, than husband hunting as her mother and aunt wished. Only the finest lords would be in attendance, and of course it was her duty to snare one. "Please, Aunt. Not today."

"This disdain you show for society cannot continue," Aunt Florence snapped. "It has been several months since Lord Jensen St. John…"

A look of discomfort crossed Aunt Florence's face, and Payton smiled tightly. It had indeed been several months since he had walked away after publicly announcing their engagement to the *haute monde*. "I feel no disdain for society, Aunt, I am simply indifferent." Payton would never admit pain still twisted her heart when she remembered how young ladies she'd believed to be friends cut her after Lord Jensen walked away.

"Well," Aunt Florence said, clearly flustered. "This indifference cannot continue. It has been made known that your father has doubled your dowry. I believe even St. John may be persuaded to walk with you again, my dear, and that would certainly make society look favorably on you."

Now was not the time to let it be known that he was already pressing his suit. "I have been jilted, and all of London blames me for it. I still cannot understand how a broken engagement suggests inferiority on my part, when it was the man who was inconstant. I do not care if I find favor with the *haute monde*."

"Let's not refer to that unpleasant time," her mother said. "Have you looked through the list of gentlemen your aunt left with you earlier? Lord Danbury is at the top of the list. I find him to be exceedingly pleasant, and he is not too old. We believe the earl to be only forty-five, and he is actively seeking a wife. "

Payton rubbed her temples, hoping to soothe the headache she could feel forming. "Do you know, Mama, how exhausting it is to be badgered *every day* for the past year? My only lot in life is not to find a husband and settle down with a brood of children. Has it never occurred to you I may want more?" she asked softly.

"To find a husband and provide his heirs *is* a woman's lot in life. Anything more is sure to breed disappointment," Aunt Florence said, a tinge of bitterness coating her tone.

Sympathy sliced through Payton's heart. Her aunt had never been able to carry a child to term, and her husband had been sorely disappointed. Her mother continually spoke of her children and husband as being her joy and the source of her comfort in life. Payton understood that was their life, but she wanted to be the engine behind hers, or she would go mad from the constant plotting and speaking of a man's money and title as if those defined what was inside his heart.

"I admit a husband would be a wonderful blessing to have, and I look forward to the day I will hold such happiness. But there is more to my life than the pursuit of a future husband and children, and I would like, for once, to speak of something else. Times have changed, mother. More young ladies are marrying at twenty-three or even older. I have at least three more years before I must…*hunt* in the marriage mart, as Aunt Florence calls courtship."

"Please do not sprout again this silly idea of yours to pen children's stories," her mother snapped, her face pinched with disapproval. "I cannot understand why you are being so difficult. I know you, Payton. You want a husband and children. Why punish yourself with the loss of them because of a misunderstanding?"

Payton's heart squeezed. "I never said I did not desire a family, Mother," she said warily. She did want her own family, but there was plenty of time to find a happy situation, and they needed to see that. Most importantly, the man she married must be as ordinary as she. He must be dependable, unpretentious, and incapable of being seduced by the opinions of high society, and he would love and appreciate all of her.

Then maybe she would trust him with her heart.

She had not been ostracized like Lord Anthony and his younger sister, Lady Constance, who had the sobriquet *the beautiful bastard*. While Payton had not been so viciously shunned, she was no longer embraced, either, and she felt as if she looked through a murky looking glass into a life of wealth, beauty, and privilege, of which she had once yearned to be a part. How foolish she had been. She was grateful she had escaped the clutches of high society, and she would never willingly place herself in their clasp again.

"Mr. Konstantinovich has invited me to picnic with him. I consented, and I will ask Lady Victoria to chaperone." A thing Payton thought unnecessary considering they would be in full view of others strolling on the lawns.

"I am certain I misheard," her mother whispered, shock evident in her tone.

"It was an offer for an outing, Mother, not one of marriage."

"He will believe it indicates a willingness on your part to walk with him," Aunt Florence said.

A deeper throb started between Payton's brows. "I said yes, and it would be discourteous of me now to decline." She would not relent, and if she were to win this argument without her mother descending into hysteria and summoning her father, then mayhap she could win the war to make her decisions with little fuss.

A boom of thunder had everyone jerking, and Payton peeked through the windows. The sky had darkened, and the trees swayed under a sharp gust of wind. It seemed as if the day would be spent indoors and the game of croquet, which had been organized, would be canceled.

"A picnic in this weather would be ill-advised," Aunt Florence said with a smirk of satisfaction.

She was unfortunately correct. Payton would take the

time to work on the illustrations for the twins' fairy tale and would do her very best not to think of Mikhail's audacious wink, her mystifying response to it, and the sense of loss she now felt because they would not be able to picnic together. Maybe it was for the best.

With a murmured excuse she swept from the parlor. She headed for the Rose Room, a very secluded and smaller drawing room Jocelyn had insisted Payton commandeer for her personal space to work. She entered, strolling to the windows to draw the golden cords for the drapes.

Oh!

Mikhail was rabble-rousing on the lawn outside with little Lord William, Jocelyn's nine-year-old brother. The boy shrieked and chortled as Mikhail ran backward to catch the ball soaring in the air. They were playing cricket. Payton stood frozen, soaking in his handsomeness and kindness. Not many would have halted their day's activities to play with children. Lady Emily, Jocelyn's thirteen-year-old sister, fisted her hands on her hips, and even from where she stood, Payton could see her bottom lip quivering.

Mikhail picked a wildflower and presented it to her with a flourish and a bow. The frown on Emily's face vanished, and delight suffused her features, and then with elegance that surprised Payton, Emily dipped into a curtsy. Payton laughed as Mikhail ruined it all by rubbing his knuckles on Emily's head. A mystified look crossed his face when Lady Emily scowled and stomped away.

She is a girl, you dolt, experiencing her first infatuation, and you just treated her like a little brother.

It was then Payton decided she would prepare to battle her parents for the right to choose a man as heartwarmingly delicious and ordinary as Mikhail. Thunder rumbled, and fat heavy drops of rain descended from the sky, slapping against the glass like pebbles. There were shrieks, and the children and several guests raced from the lawn.

Mikhail remained, tipping his head to the sky, the column of his throat displayed. The strong lines of his jaw were clean-shaven, revealing every arrogant line of his handsome features. He was dressed in dark trousers and an open-neck white linen shirt. Within seconds he was soaked, but he did not move.

Awareness stirred inside as she drank in his virile pose. The shirt plastered to his chest and, even from where she stood, she could see the sculpted hardness of his body. The need to touch him welled, and she bit the inside of her lower lip, hoping to banish the wanton thoughts. Could she draw him so—muscular legs braced apart, head tipped to the darkened sky, the corded arch of his neck begging for someone…for *her*, to glide her tongue over his skin, tasting him, and then ending the stroke of her tongue at his lips? He lowered his head and unerringly looked right at her.

Oh.

He lifted an eyebrow in challenge, and Payton's heart lurched. She froze, and they stared at each other for unending seconds. Then he scowled and walked away.

Confusion rushed through her. For a few seconds she'd thought he was just as enthralled by her. Yet now he seemed angry. Maybe it really had been the best thing for the rain to ruin their chance to picnic. For if she was not careful she could once again lead her fanciful heart to pain and disappointment.

Chapter Six

Mikhail surged to wakefulness, his heart thundering in his chest, phantom pain and pleasure twisting through his gut like acid. It had been years since he'd woke in such a state, and he knew what—or better *who* had caused it—Payton. She made him feel. Her expression as she'd watched him through the windows had been one of yearning. It had been so intense, something primal in Mikhail had unfurled, and the desire to really know her had rushed to the fore.

Who was she really?

For what did she hunger?

What made her happy?

The depth of anger he'd felt at his weakness burned beneath his skin even now. How was it possible he was not able to control the cravings running amok in his body? After being used for Madam Anya's depraved pleasures, the depth of self-loathing that had filled him because his body had responded against his will had nearly crippled him. He'd dragged himself from the void and had mastered his body's reactions. But somehow, he was inexplicably unable to bury the need Payton was calling forth.

If he was honest, he would admit he was anticipating seeing her again.

He'd tried to connect on an intimate level with Lady Olga after Madam Anya, and the coldness that had rushed through his soul had manifested outward. No pleadings or overtures of affections had been able to soften him. Since then he'd not made any effort to attempt what was deemed normalcy. It was inevitable for the same thing to happen with Payton if he pursued her. She was not a light-skirt for casual dalliances, so he could not seduce her to simply slake his lust; she would be a conquest for marriage.

He pushed from the bed and strolled to the wide Palladian windows. Moonlight bathed the land in an ethereal glow, tempting him to exit the house and take a midnight swim in the lake.

The freezing water would help him clear his head.

With quick movements, he drew on his trousers and tugged a simple shirt from the armoire. He wasted no time slipping his feet into shoes. He opened the door and padded silently along the darkened corridor, then down the winding staircase. The quiet of the house was soothing, and memories of running down these steps with Sebastian and Anthony had Mikhail smiling.

A light wavered in the distance, and he stopped. Sherring Cross was a large estate, and Mikhail's chamber was well secluded from the rest of the guests. There should be no one up and about in the west wing where his chamber was located. The light appeared closer, and he saw it was a candle flame. Who else would be awake at this hour?

He pressed forward and descended the stairs. The light from the candle was not enough to penetrate the overwhelming dark, and he could not make out the features of the person climbing the steps. The flapping voluminous white nightgown indicated a woman. A faint scent of berries had his nostril flaring. A hiss slipped from beneath his teeth.

He kept his steps light and soundless, while she clambered up the stairs with enough noise to wake the dead. It took him a while to realize she was muttering beneath her breath.

He waited for her to realize he was a mere six steps above her.

"Oh!" She dropped the candelabrum, and darkness enclosed them. There was a flurry of sounds as she rapidly descended the stairs, running from him.

To her credit she had not screamed. But was she not afraid of tripping?

He grabbed the banister and followed. "My apologies, I did not mean to startle you."

Her footsteps halted. "Mik…Mr. Konstantinovich?"

"I thought we had dispensed with formalities, Payton."

A whisper of sound rode the air, and he could feel that she moved closer. Common sense insisted he retreat, but he stood rooted, waiting for her to re-climb the steps.

"You made me drop my light." Her tone rang with accusation.

"I had not thought you would be so easily frightened."

She snorted, and a reluctant smile tugged at his lips. Had he ever heard a lady snort? Surely such a sound must be in his realm of experience. Yet the only ones he could remember were sweet giggles, simpers, and lustful moans.

"I thought you were…"

Her voice petered, and he frowned. Was she partaking in a tryst? As far as he knew no other guest resided in this section of the house.

His gut clenched in denial. "Who did you think I was?" His tone was too harsh. The quick emotions she roused were unsettling. He raked his fingers through his hair and inhaled. "Forgive my tone; I have no right to make demands."

A light laugh came from her, and he thought he detected nervousness, or was it embarrassment? She muttered something too low for him to decipher.

"What?"

A heavy sigh. "I thought you could have been the ghost I was writing about earlier."

A ghost? "I see." Except he did not see. "Would you care to inform me why you were skulking around this side of the house?"

A low feminine growl of affront resounded. "Must I redirect the question so we can assess who was really *skulking*?"

He was beginning to realize she detested the word "skulk." "My chamber is located at the fifth door on the landing."

"Oh!"

Why had he given her the precise location?

"I thought this side of the manor was vacant."

Her unique scent of berries wafted even closer, and he could just about make out the white of her robe. Her heat brushed against him, and he froze. *Too close.* Yet he did not step back.

"I am writing a story about a few children hunting a ghost in a place similar to Sherring Cross, so I waited until the house quieted before I decided to conduct some research in the wing I thought empty. I never expected to find you…skulking."

There was no disguising the amusement in her tone, and he finally allowed himself a smile. "Research?" he prompted, beyond curious.

"Yes, I wanted a greater feel of the fright the children would experience. Seeing you standing on the stairs like Barnabas gave me a great appreciation."

"Barnabas?"

"The ghost." Laughter lurked in her tone.

Of course. He wanted to see her so badly it was an ache.

Was her hair unbound? Pinned in a loose knot? Were her eyes glittering with awareness or apprehension? "Would you like to continue?"

"Touring the west wing?" Surprise tinged her voice.

"Yes."

A sharp inhalation. "It would be shamelessly inappropriate for me to agree."

He grunted.

Then silence.

Shuffling sounds crept into the still of the night. "What are you doing?"

"I am looking for the candelabrum. I would hate for you to trip over it and break your neck."

He smiled. "Leave it; I will locate it in the morning. Do you wish to continue on the tour?"

Mikhail swore he could feel her thinking.

"It would take too much to return to my chamber for a wick," she finally answered.

"I would be your guide. I am familiar with this wing… intimately." What the hell was wrong with him? Why was he not pushing her away?

She sighed, and it caressed against his skin. Suddenly he wanted her to touch him, if only to see if he would feel revulsion. "Payton?"

"I…I am tempted, but I do not think it is wise."

He was damn glad one of them was capable of sound reasoning.

"But I would appreciate your company on the return journey."

Tension eased from his shoulders. "Then you shall have it."

"Thank you."

Then unexpectedly she reached out and grasped his arm. Dread rolled over him like a dark tide. The burn of it was so cold, his teeth almost chattered. Though he did not break out in a cold sweat, nor had nausea churned in his gut, Mikhail snatched his arm away, and she stumbled. He caught her at the hips, and her gasp traveled through him at their too-close embrace.

"Are you well?"

"Yes."

He gently pressed his thumb along her side. She shivered, the softest of moans slipping from her.

"Do you suffer any ill effect from the fall?" he asked gruffly, pulling away.

She sighed. "There is only a slight bruise. The pain has already faded."

"Good. You should still rub the area with a liniment." He took her arm and placed it on the railing of the stairs. Then he nudged her.

They descended the steps carefully.

"Did you receive my note expressing my regret for missing our picnic?" she asked.

"I did." He'd still not figured out if the rain had been a timely or untimely intervention. The gentlemanly thing to do would be to offer an invitation for another day, but he remained silent.

They reached the bottom of the stairs.

"A moment, Payton."

She halted, and he felt along the wall for a switch. He located it, twisted the knob, and soft light illuminated the corridor.

"I would prefer for the light to be off. I know I am being frightfully improper, but I would like to continue my research. I think I will also insert in the story the children dropping their torches," she said excitedly. "I want to see what their walk with darkness would be like. It is very convenient for me that you are here now. I would hate to encounter the real

Barnabas alone."

With a low chuckle he complied, and they kept walking, hugging close to the wall. "So tell me about Barnabas."

She stopped so suddenly his chest pressed into her back, and the curve of her rump pressed delightfully against his thigh. He bit back a groan and gently eased away.

"You want to know about my writing?" Her voice was rife with surprise.

"I do." He frowned, a peculiar ache working its way into his chest. Was his request so unusual?

"Oh!"

Pleasure coated her voice, and he wished to see her face. Was she smiling?

"I am not certain if he is a mean or a kind ghost as yet. But it is wartime, and four sibling children are sent away to live with their grandparents and discover the castle they are living in is haunted."

He smiled, wondering if she realized her voice had lowered to a dramatic hush.

"Tell me from the beginning," he commanded as they continued strolling in the dark.

A little squeak of excitement slipped from her, and then she launched into the story she was writing and apparently illustrating—a ghost, a mystical portal, an enchanted realm with dragons, witches, trolls, a red queen, a blue queen, and intrepid children, all woven together seamlessly into a wonderful story. Her voice was refined and sensual, soothing and arousing, and she entranced him with the passion vibrating from her as she regaled him until the tale ended.

He was silent for a few seconds. "Your story is riveting."

"Thank you for listening," she said softly.

Much too soon, they reached the foyer leading to the other wing of the manor. The light from the wall sconces lighting the east wing bared her to his gaze. She was dressed in a voluminous nightgown that hid her wonderful figure, and her hair was pinned in a topknot. Loose tendrils danced around her flushed cheeks, her eyes glittered with apparent delight, and Mikhail desperately wanted to taste her lips.

He cleared his throat. "This is where we part."

She lowered her lashes, but not before he saw the sparks of desire in her eyes. She pinned a polite smile on her face, and then lifted her gaze to his. "Thank you for being so kind as to escort me and listen to me ramble."

"I was delighted."

Her flush became even more pronounced. She reached out and briefly touched his knuckle. Her caress was light as butterfly wings and *almost* pleasant. Then she turned and ran lightly up the winding staircase.

Mikhail watched until she vanished from sight. She was a powerful temptation he would have to do all in his power to resist. Then the visceral need of how he'd wanted her lips against his, the way she'd made his cock twitch, the way she made him smile so effortlessly, scythed through his heart.

And her touch…it had not made his gut roil with the urge to vomit. A part of him that had been dead and buried whispered through his soul. Maybe this time, he could take a step off the cliff of insanity and triumph.

Chapter Seven

The next morning Payton entered the stables with eager steps. It was very early, but she'd wanted to escape the after breakfast call to play croquet. Her damnable need to see Mikhail had made her restless. Last night had been thrilling. Nothing had happened except a long walk along a darkened corridor, but she'd had more enjoyment than at the dinner and the dance earlier. She liked him, and she could not deny the need to be in his presence despite the caution that flared in her heart. The last thing she wanted was to endure hurt and disappointment again.

A cursory glance showed the stables to be empty, and disappointment stabbed through her. It was a bit ridiculous and improper of her, but she had wanted to see Mikhail without the prying eyes of the other guests upon them. What she would say when she actually saw the man, she had not thought of as yet.

She directed her thoughts to the stallion she'd ridden yesterday, moving with rapidity to his stall.

Payton faltered. *Mikhail*. He wore a gentleman's white

shirt tucked into perfectly fitted black trousers; his black hair was mussed and in need of a trim. Though he groomed the horse, he had an imperious bearing about him, and it filled her with curiosity.

"Hello," she greeted.

He stiffened imperceptibly and then shifted in her direction. His gaze ran over her in a quick perusal, and Payton realized she had carefully dressed in the event they had a chance encounter. Clad in her finest green riding habit, with matching gloves and hat, she warmed at the appreciation glowing in his eyes.

"Good day, Payton." His accent was so appealing.

"Did you return safely to the west wing without mishap?"

"I did."

She moved closer to the stall. "I am glad to see Sage returned safely."

"He did."

She waited for him to say something more, anything really to prolong their conversing. A blush climbed her neck when he only stared in that piercing way of his.

"It is a glorious day for riding."

He glanced through the open windows into the sky. "It is."

"The duchess's sister, Lady Victoria, has organized a game of croquet to be played on the front lawn," Payton said, strolling closer. "Then later a game of charades in the parlor. I am stealing away to ride across the countryside."

He arched a brow.

"Will you be joining the games?" she asked. However, when she thought of it, she realized he might not have been invited.

"No."

God, she hoped she didn't make him feel inferior with her question. It could not be pleasant to realize all other guests had been encouraged to play. Payton had felt the sting of rejection many times since the Viscountess of Kenilworth organized social events and made it her duty to not invite Payton, taking pleasure in reminding her of her inferior rank. "I am sorry you did not receive an invitation."

"I was invited."

"Oh! I feel foolish for making such an assumption." She laughed lightly, more from the discomfort curling through her than anything else.

He grunted.

That is it?

She waited for him to say more, but he remained maddeningly silent. She glanced around the stables, admiring the elegant lines and beauty of the other horses. She walked away from him, toward a horse with the blackest coat she had ever beheld. Another stallion. "Oh, you beauty," she crooned gently, reaching out to glide her fingertip over his muscles. "Will you allow me to ride you today?"

He nickered, and she laughed softly, moving close until she could press against his side, running her hand along his neck. Her heart quickened. She could feel Mikhail's eyes upon her. The intensity of his gaze kissed over her in a heated caress, an invitation to shift and admire him in a similar manner. But that would be too bold, too blatantly outrageous, even for her. Payton swallowed and battled the urge. Seconds passed in silence while she allowed the horse to become familiar with her touch. She swore the blasted man stared at her the entire time. Unable to resist, she turned to Mikhail.

His regard was…provocative. His eyes lowered to her lips and stayed there. Was it that she had something on her mouth? *Good Lord*, what if crumbles from the sweet cake she had stolen on her way out were still on her lips. A quick dart of her tongue along her lips did not result in anything. He frowned darkly, and awareness simmered through Payton.

"You are not much of a conversationalist today," she said

in desperation, wanting to break the intensity of the moment.

"I was uncommonly talkative in the cottage."

She frowned. "You were?" He had been reserved last night as well. She'd done most of the talking.

Silence.

"You are staring, Mikhail."

"I already informed you why I stare."

"It is ungentlemanly and outrageous."

"You enjoy the knowledge that I find you irresistibly beautiful. Do not pretend otherwise."

Irresistibly beautiful? She ignored the rush of pleasure and glared at him. "Are you trying to provoke me?"

Finally a gorgeous smile curved his lips. "No, but it was worth your pique to see your face flushed with passion. You are becoming."

Her aunt would encourage her to upbraid his boldness, but Payton could not bring herself to act so pompously. She would simply refuse to acknowledge his audacious compliment and his ridiculous assertions, which, if she were honest, held a miniscule amount of truth. It was indeed thrilling he found her becoming.

She turned to the horse she'd been admiring. "This is a beautiful horse."

"He is."

She allowed an exaggerated sigh to escape her. "I can see you are not fit for company today."

He grunted and then asked, "Would you like to ride him?"

A smile split her face. "Indeed I would."

He walked over and with quick movements fitted the stallion with saddle and harness. "This is Aeton. He is well trained and responds without the urging of a riding crop."

"I would never use a crop!"

Mikhail flashed a smile of approval. "Good. He can be a bit temperamental, but once you let him know you are in charge, he will respond to your guidance."

"And you trust me with him?"

"From what I saw yesterday your skill is beyond reproach."

Warmth filled her chest. "Thank you," she said softly. Not many men would offer such a compliment, and she knew none who would encourage a young lady to mount a stallion. Even Calydon encouraged his unconventional duchess to ride mares, never a powerful beast like Aeton. "Did you train him?"

"I did."

"You are a horse breeder and a man of affairs. A very curious combination."

He stiffened, then relaxed his shoulders. "I breed horses as a hobby. At rare times I gift them to friends."

"And Aeton is a gift to Calydon?"

"He is."

"And what other hobbies do you pursue?"

He stepped from the horse and directed his undivided attention to her. "You are curious about me." More of an observation than a question.

Though his face was shuttered, pleasure darkened his tone. She hesitated. *Never be obvious in your tendre for a gentleman.* With an inner snort, she dismissed her aunt's instructions. "I am," she said truthfully. His silent regard became unsettling as a disconcerting awareness of him rippled over her skin. "If you are uncomfortable speaking—"

"Would you allow me to accompany you on your ride?"

He was bolder than any other suitor she had ever encountered. She barely contained a wince at her thoughts; a simple ride was not an invitation to courting. Or was it? She tried to remember all the infernal rules to courtship her aunt repeated so often. Payton was not sure if her curiosity should extend to being alone with him again. Not that a ride in the open should be a breach in propriety.

"We did not indulge in our picnic yesterday," he offered by way of explanation.

He strolled to Sage and started fitting his saddle, seemingly unconcerned with her answer, but Payton swore she could feel the tension rolling off Mikhail as he awaited her reply.

"I would love your company." Her heart thudded at his slow pleased smile. "I would also like to race against you with Sage."

Mikhail stared at her for so long, she almost fidgeted. Was she being too impertinent?

"I accept."

The breath she had not realized she held whooshed from her audibly. "You do?" Never had she really expected him to acquiesce. The one time she had been so daring with Lord Jensen in Hyde Park, he had been incensed that as a "lady" she would suggest racing against a gentleman.

"I do…though I must warn you, you will not win."

She narrowed her eyes, and he chuckled.

"So if you are so certain, why accept? I clearly present no challenge."

Something wicked flared in the depth of his eyes. "Oh, you challenge me," he drawled softly. "I will savor the thrill of my conquest."

Conquest? "Are we still talking about racing?"

He gave her an almost baffled look before responding. "Of course."

"I see." But she did not see, and she was almost certain he referred to something else. It was as if she should have understood a hidden meaning in his words, and he had an expectation of her to be more elegant and possibly adept at flirtation. Or maybe she was being silly. "I am an expert horsewoman even riding sidesaddle, so prepare to be trounced."

A boot crunched behind her and she spun to see a large

and very handsome man walking toward them.

"Miss Peppiwell, may I introduce you to my assistant, Vladimir."

The man's probing gaze was unsettling. His expression was guarded…cold even, and a shiver of discomfort coursed through her.

She quickly greeted him. "It is delightful to make your acquaintance, Vladimir."

The man grunted.

"By chance are you related to Mr. Konstantinovich?"

Vladimir's mien became even more distant.

"I…I only asked because Mr. Konstantinovich also has a penchant to grunt and provide one syllable answers. Please ignore my uncalled-for impertinence," she ended sweetly, not knowing what she did to elicit such an immediate dislike.

Laughter bubbled inside when the man only softly grunted. She suppressed it and moved to the mounting block to seat herself. Mikhail conferred in the corner with Vladimir. Imperious anger flashed across Mikhail's face, and his assistant bowed, handed him a basket and, with a stiff nod in her direction, departed.

The exchange had curiosity filling Payton. Mikhail watched Vladimir leave, his face not betraying any of his thoughts. Then he strode to Sage. Payton's breath hitched at the grace in which Mikhail seated his horse.

They cantered out of the stables. The gentle breeze lifted the tendrils of hair from her forehead. Payton lifted her face to the sun as it crested over the horizon and broke through the darkened clouds, breathing in the fresh crisp scent of the morning. "I do wish I was riding astride."

His eyes flicked to her. "I will wait if it is your wish to dress accordingly."

"My mother and aunt would never forgive me if I traipsed around in such garments when amongst such lofty guests," she admitted on a light laugh, nodding to the few people on the lawn playing croquet.

He nudged his horse closer. "I have seen the duchess riding in breeches."

"She is a duchess. I daresay she can do whatever she wishes without exciting malicious comments. It is not the same for a mere 'miss.'"

"And you speak from experience?"

She shrugged, unable to answer because of the sudden tightness in her throat. She did not want to delve into the disappointment and hurt she had endured. Payton would much prefer learning about him. She was no longer naive enough to trust easily but, for the first time in months, she wanted to ride and indulge in laughter and the dance of courtship with a gentleman. Her mother and Aunt Florence would be thrilled to know Payton was moving away from the pain of being jilted, but would be livid to know it was because of a mere mister. "I will admit I have stepped close to society's flame, and I felt the heat of their displeasure." More like she had been engulfed in the most painful of fires.

"I am familiar with how unforgiving society can be."

She gave him a curious smile. "I had not expected a man of affairs to be intimately acquainted with the *haute monde*."

Guilt flashed in his eyes, and he looked away from her toward the rolling countryside. "I have been deeply enmeshed in their circles for years now."

"You have?"

Piercing blue eyes swung back to her. "Yes. I thought you mentioned a race?"

"Then let us ride," she said, surging her horse ahead.

Without hesitation he tore after her.

Payton laughed in exhilaration at the magnificent speed and grace of the stallion beneath her, delighted that Mikhail was not holding back in his challenge. He was treating her as an equal and not some fragile lady to be cosseted or scolded for her boldness. Adrenaline pumped through her veins, and her heartbeat quickened as they sped past the rolling countryside, a blur of greens and the bright splash of flowers and roses. The steady sounds of hoof beats thumping the ground in a thrilling rhythm urged her to encourage her horse to move faster.

They cut the corner at breakneck speed, and delight pulsed through her veins. She rode the wind, and joy uncurled in her. The power of his stallion outdistanced hers, but she did not care. The very fact he afforded her such freedom, to be wild and daring, thrilled her to her toes.

They swept behind a cusp of trees, slowing their pace. They trotted in companionable silence before halting in a clearing behind a copse of willow trees. A faint sound of gurgling water reached her ears, along with the sweet trilling of birds. Payton could not resist the laugh that pelted from her. It was loud, boisterous, and utterly unladylike, and she did not care. "That was glorious, Mikhail. We must indulge in another race. Next time I will be properly attired, and I am certain I will trounce you."

"Your laugh…it's beautiful."

A sweet ache pulsed in her chest. A memory of chortling too loudly at an intimate garden party Lord Jensen's mother had hosted blared in Payton's mind. The viscountess had sniffed, aiming her pointy nose in the air with a caustic comment that Payton laughed like an American. Many of the other ladies had twittered and giggled behind their fans, while her cheeks had burned in mortification. Lord Jensen had not even defended her, only whispering discreetly that she should ignore them, that she was lovely, and they were simply envious.

But this man…he thought her very loud laugh was *beautiful*. She didn't want to be captivated, but he was just so intriguing. Payton wasn't sure if she should trust the feelings of interest curling through her, for it was surely the path to heartache. "When you stare at me so, what are your thoughts?" *Oh God*, she was being too bold.

He leaned forward, resting his muscular forearms on his thighs. "I think of what it would be like to dance with you, to feel your passion in movement and sounds, to taste you."

She snapped her gaze to his. "You think of kissing me?" She pushed the words out, determined to sound worldly and unaffected.

"The image has dominated my thoughts since we met." He sounded disgruntled.

Desire brushed against her senses. *I have imagined kissing you as well.* Never would she confess such a scandalous thought, but from the smile curving his lips, it was as if he knew her most intimate musings.

"Come, let us eat."

"Eat?" she parroted inanely. It was then she saw the small basket tied securely behind him. "I do not think, after our vigorous race, the food will be edible. You had intended to picnic alone?"

His mouth twitched. "No."

"So sure of me were you?"

"More like desperately hopeful."

She laughed lightly, loving his utterance. *Desperately hopeful.* "I see, and what is our fare?"

"I coaxed Calydon's cook to make us something special."

"You have a unique relationship with the duke. You have an entire wing of Sherring Cross at your disposal and now his cook," she teased.

"I have known him for years." He dismounted and assisted her to the ground, careful to leave space between their bodies.

"He seems a generous employer if he allows you to coax his cook. Though I can imagine with just a smile you would have Mrs. Beaton willing to make anything for you."

"Ah…is this your way of telling me that with a smile I can have you at my whim?"

"Absolutely not, it would take more beguilement than a mere smile to charm me. I am made of sterner stuff."

His soft laugh brushed against her skin like temptation itself, and he was so darkly seductive he took Payton's breath.

In silence they walked farther into the clearing, approaching a small brook. Gray clouds hovered above the sky, and a distant thunder rumbled. The day was so beautiful she prayed rain did not interrupt. In the center there was a stone table and chair. Mikhail unpacked the food on the table. A wine and some sort of confectionary.

"What is that?"

"It's *halva*, made with almond. Try it," he invited as they sat.

She took a delicate bite. Her eyes widened at the delicious flavors exploding along her taste buds. "This is wonderful."

He had a bottle and two small glasses which he filled with a golden liquid. "This is *Medovukha*. I am fortunate to have an assistant who knows how to make it."

She accepted the proffered glass and took a tentative sip. It was impossible to hold back the moan of pleasure. "That really is wonderful."

"Now you'll understand why Vladimir, though grouchy, is invaluable to me."

They drank and ate in companionable silence, and Payton wondered when she had ever felt such peace. Endless days of attending balls and picnics had only ever filled her with anxiety, as she'd constantly fretted if she was doing the right thing. Had she walked gracefully enough? Giggled like a lady enough, wielded her fan the proper way? Had she waited until someone was introduced before speaking? Those days had been painful…yet there had also been the thrill of just being *there* amongst such nobility.

"Do you live in England?" Mikhail asked. "Or are you only visiting?"

Payton swallowed her last piece of *halva*. "I may eventually return to Boston, but for now I am firmly rooted here."

"You do not sound too happy."

She considered her words carefully. "There are wonderful things in England. I have been much exposed to arts and books, which I adore, more so than when I lived in America. I simply do not feel like I fit, and there are times I despise attending society functions."

"Then why do you attend?"

"It is very difficult to refuse my mother or aunt or even my father. Not that I think I will be banished as my mother threatens, but I am subjected to their whims by law until I reach my majority."

With a sigh she rose to her feet and walked along the edge of the small brook. "I do understand they wish for me to make an advantageous match and to be comfortably situated. But I believe there is more to life than being the wife of a lord."

He stood and moved to stand beside her. He was close, the warmth of him reaching out and gliding against her skin. But she did not move away, in fact, she subtly swayed closer. "What about you, Mikhail? Will you return to Russia?"

"I will visit my family yearly, but my home is now in England."

She heard the wistfulness in his tone, and she understood. A day had not passed that she did not reminisce on Boston, the life and friends she had left there. "And will you settle here in Norfolk?"

"For now."

She waited for him to expound, but he remained silent. Payton hesitated to pry further, though the need to learn more about him was becoming a persistent desire. "Do you have a wife?"

Startled eyes met hers. "I would not dream of tasting you if I were attached."

She flushed. "Of course. I did not think you without honor, I…I…merely wondered if you had any attachment, and I asked the question poorly."

"I had an understanding once, but we agreed we would not suit."

There was a dark undertone in his voice that had her assessing him carefully. "May I ask why?"

He grimaced. "The fault lies with me. She understandably needed more from me, and I was unable to provide it."

She touched his arms lightly, and he froze. She quickly withdrew her fingers, a blush heating her cheeks. "Such a separation must have caused you pain. I am sorry."

"It was years ago; if it caused pain, I have forgotten," he said in a voice that was chillingly distant.

Awareness of how secluded they were reared its head. She strolled toward the grazing horses, and he kept pace with her, each of his steps exuding masculine grace and vitality. "Thank you for riding with me. I must return to the estate. I am to be fitted for a ball gown for Lady Blythe's midnight soiree this weekend. My mother would lambast me if I missed the modiste the duchess has been kind enough to ask to attend our needs."

He nodded. "Reserve a spot for me on your dance card."

Liquid warmth slid through her veins. "You will attend?"

"Yes."

An event she had previously dreaded now had anticipation curling through her. "I am surprised." He arched a brow, and she winced. "Please do not think me unkind. I only know the bigotry of society and had not thought Lady Blythe would have invited you to her ball."

"Think nothing of causing me offense; I much prefer if you speak freely. My connection with Calydon allows me much within society."

Of course. It was the same connection her family shamelessly importuned upon. Was it that he yearned to be a part of the *haute monde*? A sinking sensation entered her stomach. "I see."

"The disappointment in your tone compels me to know what it is you believe you have perceived."

"I had the thought you might wish to be a part of the coveted inner circles of the *haute monde*. The idea disappointed me, when it should not have. I have no right to judge you based on my desires."

His gaze settled on her face. "And your desire is not to be associated with high society?"

Payton hesitated. "Yes."

The twig between his fingers snapped. "May I enquire as to what happened?"

She hesitated. "I don't belong. Months after being introduced to society I waited for someone to look at me and see the dirt beneath my fingernails."

She held up her hands, and he lightly encircled her wrists.

"These hands have milked a cow and dug deep into the soil. They have even scrubbed a pot and lifted a chamber pot."

Amusement gleamed in his eyes. He pulled her fingers toward his lips and brushed the lightest of a kiss across the tips. Payton wasn't sure if she should pull from his caress or lean farther in to him. She glanced through the trees, unable to make out the indistinct forms of the players on the lawn. But if she could see them, surely they could see a man and a woman standing much too close.

"Industrious hands are not dirty, they are to be much admired," he murmured.

"Sentiments only few would agree with."

"What else has contributed to your distaste of high society?"

"Many young ladies I had thought close acquaintances took pleasure in reminding me I did not belong to their social circles. I ignored my discomfort, my sister's warnings of the hypocritical nature of society, and enjoyed each lavish ball I attended. The heir to a viscountcy pursued me most ardently and I…believed I loved him."

Mikhail's expression became guarded, but Payton knew he held on to her every word. There was a piercing stillness about him that unsettled her, and his grip had tightened reflexively on her fingers.

"Do you still love him?"

"I do not think so."

His expression became even more closed, and her heart thudded.

"What happened with this man?"

She pulled her fingers from his clasp, a bit thrown by his intensity. "He proposed to me, and our engagement was announced. A rumor started circulating concerning someone close to my family, and society was very cruel in their reactions. I was tarnished by association, and Lord Jensen withdrew his affections."

And society blamed me, hated me, and cut me for it, because it was further proof of my inferiority. The unspoken words were still too painful for her to admit.

"He was a damn fool. A mere rumor would not dissuade me from your charms."

Pleasure suffused her at Mikhail's assertions. "Thank you for your kind words."

"I did not offer them out of kindness."

Her breath hitched at the shadows of hunger in his eyes, and she swallowed at the startling throb in her lower stomach. *Not good.* While she liked him, her family would object. But did she care? She *liked* him. "I have never had anyone look at me as you do," she said softly. "Your gaze is like a physical touch; its intensity is almost alarming."

A fleeting smile touched his lips. "I will learn to temper my attraction."

"I would urge you not to." Her voice was a mere whisper, but from the flash of desire that darkened his eyes, he had heard. He leaned in, and for a heart-stopping moment she thought he would kiss her. *Please.* She wanted the press of his mouth against hers.

"Your lips have been haunting me."

"I am sorry to have caused you misery," she said teasingly, trying to rein in the ridiculous need to behave wantonly.

He placed his hands on her hips, drawing her closer to his delicious warmth. "More like tormenting me."

"Then I am sorry if I have caused you pain," she whispered as she lifted her arms and clasped his shoulder. Acting on pure feminine instinct, she pressed her nose in to his neck, breathing in his evocative scent.

He froze, and a chill blasted her. A fraught silence settled around them, the undercurrents of something unknown rippling across Payton's skin. The chill seemed to gather in strength, and she could feel him retreating, though he did not move. It scared her.

Instinctively she dropped her hands from his shoulders. Tension visibly drained from his body when she stepped away, and hurt lanced through her. "You find my touch repellent?" The idea seemed farfetched, but it was the alarming conclusion she had drawn.

Caution clouded his gaze. "No...never."

Soft relief pulsed, and she smiled. "For a moment I—"

"I find all touch uncomfortable," he admitted with evident discomfort.

But he seems so self-assured and arrogant...

"Oh!" She made to move away, but he gripped her hips and drew her to him. "I thought you found touching distasteful."

"If I am the one in control it does not bother me," he said in a deceptively mild tone, drawing her even closer, flushing her chest to his.

Oh.

"I have an incurable love for horses and dogs. I enjoy archery and boxing."

She lifted her eyes to his, and the heat in his gaze strangled her breathing. "I…I feel as if you are about to kiss me, so for you to talk of dogs, horses, and pugilistic skills in this moment is decidedly confusing."

His fingers tangled in her hair, and he lifted her face even closer. "You'd asked about my hobbies. What about yours?"

The anticipation of feeling his lips and tasting them for the first time was burning away all her resistance to mere ashes, and he wanted to *converse*?

He pressed a kiss to the corner of her mouth, darting his tongue to caress the closed seam of her lips. Payton's knees weakened.

"I am a terrible painter," she said huskily. "But I love to see images I create come to life on a canvas. You already know I enjoy writing fairy tales and drawing the images that roar to life in my mind to accompany my stories."

"I look forward to reading them."

Her breath hitched as nerves fluttered inside her. He pressed kisses to her lips. Payton sighed, loving the firm pressure on her mouth.

"You taste very sweet," he murmured.

"It is the *halva*."

He trailed his lips to the corner of her mouth and licked his tongue in a wicked and sensual glide of shocking temptation across the seam of her closed lips. "No…it is you." He bit her lower lip and tugged, sliding his tongue inside.

She jerked in shock.

"It is definitely you," he said, his voice low and gravelly. "You are testing my control, and I ache to taste you deeper."

She had no sensible response as confusing heat suffused her entire body.

He bent to nibble at her throat, the teasing strokes of his tongue rousing sensations she had never felt before. Everything inside of Payton ached. Her breasts and her most intimate valley throbbed, and she desperately wanted his touch, his taste, anything to relieve the sweet unknown pressure building.

"Then savor me," she invited with a purr as he nipped the sensitive hollow of her throat.

He trailed fleeting kisses up to her lips, then teased her mouth in a seductive caress as she opened farther for him, inviting him inside.

"I can taste your innocence," he growled softly.

"Is that so terrible?"

"It is dangerous, for I hunger for things you are too innocent to give."

Then he stung her bottom lip with another sensuous nip. She gasped, and he coaxed with soft bites and licks at her lips, persuading her to open fully to his entreaty, then a beat later Mikhail claimed her in a show of raw dominance.

Flames of desire consumed her.

It was both…gently marauding and savagely ravishing. She parted her lips. A deep groan rumbled from Mikhail, and he kissed her deeper. His tongue sweeping inside her mouth was unexpected, as well as the sharp pleasure that stabbed low in her womb.

She pulled from him, panting. "I…this feels so…" Her words drifted away on a moan, as he trailed his lips over the pulse fluttering at her throat.

"Hot…needy?"

She had not realized people's lips and tongue could mesh so delightfully. "Yes."

"Good." Then he tugged her closer, so she felt every hard inch of him, and took her lips in the same move.

Desires erupted in her unlike any she had ever known, and Payton slid deeper into sheer bliss. He owned her sighs, her moans. The kiss deepened, grew hungrier.

He pulled his lips from hers, breathing raggedly. "You intrigue me, Payton."

Delightful shock coursed through her. "I do?"

He pressed kisses along the sensitive column of her neck. "Yes, I hunger to know you."

His answer sent a shiver of uncertainty over her. He was everything that was sensual and forbidden.

"Will you allow me to take you on a walk or even a carriage ride?"

Oh.

"Payton?"

He made her heart jerk, her blood heated. *Dangerous.* So dangerously glorious and wonderful.

"You want to woo me?" She meant to ask the question teasingly, instead, her voice hitched.

"Yes."

"You hardly know me."

"I know enough."

So do I.

A wicked tension wove around them as he awaited her answer. She hated being so honest with him, but he needed to understand what he would face. "Your status is not elevated enough for my mother or father to agree to me even strolling in the gardens with you. I would hate for you to face their censure and derision."

"Is that your only objection?"

Mikhail made her want to rebel against the bidding of her family. *Good Lord, what am I thinking?* "*I* have no objection," she said softly.

He wanted to know her better, even woo her. She'd always thought she would tread with utmost caution with the next man to attempt courtship, because there was a chance her heart could once again be mangled and crushed, and the very idea was unbearable. But with Mikhail she did not want to restrain any part of herself, and the intensity of feelings roiling through her so soon was almost frightening.

"I enjoy your company, Mikhail. If my parents agree to me walking with you, I would love to get to know you more."

Pleasure flared in his eyes, then caution. Before she could question it, he tugged her closer, claiming her lips.

And even if they do not, I am determined to choose my own path.

Chapter Eight

Payton Peppiwell was delightful. Raw pleasure blasted through Mikhail at the realization she would welcome him getting to know her, despite the fact he presented himself to her as common. She desired him…simply for *him*. The knowledge was perplexingly wonderful.

Unable to stop touching her, he explored her mouth thoroughly, and the onslaughts of sensations were overwhelming. The rasping glide of her tongue against his nearly drove him to his knees. She was both sweetness and fire. She released a throaty sensual sigh, and her soft voluptuous curves melted into his hardness. He pulled from her, littering small kisses across her cheek. He bit the curve of her throat, fighting the raging need to devour her.

He thrived on control, and she tested every tether he'd placed on his passions.

"Please, Mikhail, I ache."

Need flashed through him. He allowed himself to drown in the scent and taste of her, devouring her lips with a hunger he had never felt in his existence. She purred in his mouth, responding to his embrace with ravenous fervor.

He could kiss her forever and not need anything more to sustain him. The sweet and spicy flavor of her kisses enslaved him, for he never wanted to relinquish the pleasure of her lips.

Mikhail pulled from her, breathing raggedly. The pulse fluttered at the base of her throat, her skin flushed, and her eyes had deepened to dark gold.

Lust curled through Mikhail. He wanted her underneath him. *Now*. It was much too soon, so he ruthlessly buried the need to whisk her to the stone bench and have his way with her. She was not a conquest for mere pleasure or to satiate his lust; he wanted to learn her desires and see if he could bear her touch.

Slow down.

Her face was suffused with pure gratification, and the beauty of it beguiled him. His hunger increased to a painful craving.

Touch me…please.

The visceral need to feel her hands on him increased, jerking him out of the haze of lust trying to cloud his mind. *Too soon.* "Step away," he urged. It was not in his willpower to do it himself.

She stepped back, her eyes wide with apprehension. "You must think me wanton," she said, color dusking her face.

"Honesty is rare, even in passion."

His words were a jarring punch to his system. His intention today had been to learn more about her, and though he barely scratched her surfaced, he saw much to be admired. He could not keep pretending he was a man without connections when he wanted to explore knowing her, but a vise of caution gripped his heart at the thought of revealing his titles. The peace he so desperately needed would vanish into thin air, and the hounds of society would start nipping at his heels.

Unless he asked her to keep his confidence. Would she?

He shook his head in disbelief. He'd made her acquaintance only two days past and here he was thinking to go against every experience he'd endured and take her into his confidence.

Hell.

How was it possible for her to drive him to such distraction in this short span of time? He tried to draw upon the emotionless state that had saved him countless times and was infuriatingly unable to. He wanted to confide in her. *Utter madness.* How would he even explain his secrecy without opening himself to deep questions of his past? Any revelation in that direction was not something he would allow, not now, mayhap never, and he did not want to hurt her with evasiveness.

This is why I've avoided such intimacies. Blasted hell.

One more day, he swore inwardly. *One day.* He would give himself today to see if what was burgeoning between them was worth fighting for. Then, when he was certain of *something*, he would reveal his secrets and inform her of his relation to Calydon and the realm…and his scandals.

With a sigh he pressed a kiss to her forehead, and she flowed into his embrace. It was then Mikhail realized how much he was touching her. Never had he allowed himself to be so free with a lady. He'd had an understanding with Lady Olga, and the most he'd bestowed on her were chaste kisses. She'd not tempted him to do more. Everything about Payton was smashing all of his walls to cinders.

Touch me, he urged silently, desperate to see if a prolonged touch would cause nausea to churn in his gut, or would he want to feel her fingertips gliding over his skin, rousing sensations he had not felt in ten long, cold years? Ice formed beneath his skin. Memories of dozens of unwanted hands, both man and woman, coasting over his flesh, kissing and biting, punishing and pleasuring in equal measure, had him gritting his teeth against the lurid images.

"Do you have a large family?"

Payton's question helped center him, and he latched on to the direction of her conversation gratefully. "Two brothers and my parents are alive."

"Are they in England as well?"

"No."

She looked at him, awaiting a response, but he did not want to outright lie to her. The less information he provided the better. He gritted his teeth as sourness coated his gut. He hated only confiding parts of his life to her. He should not be surprised. He hated deception in all forms and, not surprisingly, he despised it in himself, even if he hungered for solitude. The urge to reveal his wealth and status welled inside, and he had to ruthlessly push it down. "I have cousins in England, but the core of my family resides in Russia."

"Would they be pleased with you wanting to court me?"

"Why would they not be?"

Her chin went up a notch. "I am untitled and an American. Though you are similarly untitled, they may wish a greater elevation for you with an English lady."

Whenever she referred to him as ordinary it set his teeth on edge. "They will respect my choice. Above all my family wishes for my happiness, not for me to form connections."

Concern creased her brow, and she stepped away from him and walked to the stone bench and sat. "My family will not be very understanding, and I must be forthright with you…my mother and aunt will be very rude."

He sat beside her, and she leaned in to him so their shoulders brushed. Sweet pleasure twisted in Mikhail. There was no need in him to jerk away from her. In fact, he would have liked if she rested her head against his shoulder. "I have the skin of a walrus," he said softly, in awe of the needs surfacing in his soul.

She laughed, the sound husky yet musical, and some of the tension released from her. "I only wanted to prepare you. My father may be more amiable. But my mother and aunt are very determined that I marry a lord, and they will see a simple turn in the gardens with a man like you threatening to their ambitions. But I confess nothing would ever move me to such a union."

Mikhail's mind blanked for long seconds, and something akin to panic clawed from the back of his throat. He pushed it down and narrowed in on the evident pain she tried to bury. It could not have been easy being jilted and facing the censure of society. "Not all men are dishonorable, and those who are belong to both high and low society in equal measure."

Her eyes flashed fire, and she held up her hand. "I have met many lords, and I daresay I can say with confidence I know less than five men who are *true* gentlemen. At first I was coveted for my wealth, maybe my beauty, but never for my intelligence and accomplishments. After I was jilted I received several invitations from men to be their mistresses. My worth was lowered in their eyes because one of their own no longer thought I was suitable for marriage. I will admit being a part of the *haute monde* was exciting initially, but then I realized it would never end—the balls, the gossip, the careful masking of oneself so as not to offend. As long as I married a man of the *haute monde*...I too would be subject to their infernal rules and hypocrisy."

Understanding scythed through him. Most of his appeal was because he presented as common. She really had no interest in his wealth, or that he was seemingly connected to as notable a family as the Calydons. The notion was so startling it rendered Mikhail silent and, instead of filling him with pleasure, unease settled heavy in his gut. He had never met a young lady who did not yearn for a title. The entire success of their coming out in society depended on securing an advantageous match, the loftier the title the better, the more yearly income the better.

"And what would be your opinion of me, if I confessed to possessing several titles and that I am far wealthier than most of the lords you know?" He kept the tension from his voice, hoping she would view his question as mild curiosity.

She lifted startled golden eyes to his and then chuckled. "I would urge you to reconsider calling on me for, though your kisses are sublimely wonderful, I yearn for a life without the glitter of high society."

He clenched his jaw against her assertions, burying the snarl of denial. Her words were said teasingly, but her voice rang with sincerity. "You must yearn for wealth," he murmured, his heart beating more frantically than he would like. He was a damn prince. He should be cool and unflappable at all times.

"I do not."

"Damn it to hell." The snarl ripped from him, and she jerked, her eyes widening.

"Mikhail, I—"

"No…tell me what it is that you want from life. What do you need? A title or a lack of title does not define a man or a relationship. Whether I am the blasted king, or the poorest of commoner, you would have expectations of me…as a man, as *your* man. Tell me what those expectations are," he ended hoarsely, unable to tolerate the idea that the only woman he'd ever wanted, ever craved to feel her touch, would reject him because of his blasted titles. The feelings of wanting something more had been tentative, but now the thought of really experiencing a life more profound, and not encased in an emotionless shell, made his teeth ache with the need to attain.

I want to know how to please you, to chain you to me, so when I reveal my nobility you will see that you will want for nothing.

A streak of rebellion glowed in her eyes. "I want to wear trousers and ride in London if I wish without judgment. Connie's husband, the Duke of Mondvale, owns the gaming club Decadence, and I confessed to wanting to see inside. I was scolded as if I were a child and not a woman who could speak her mind and offer her opinions freely. I want to be loved…admired…respected for all I am, and not be ridiculed if I push the boundaries of the conventions instituted by a hypocritical society."

She gave a disdainful sniff. "I do not want to be told I cannot because I am not a man. Do you know how frustrating it is to never be able to feel as if I have choices? In the quiet moments when I spoke of wanting to write, I was scoffed at. When I showed my illustrations I was looked down on, not celebrated as I had hoped."

Her golden eyes flashed as she shifted on the bench to face him fully, leaning so close their lips brushed. "I…I…want to kiss you, to feel your hands on my bare skin, teasing and caressing me, and not feel as if I am wanton to indulge in such a desire."

Her words were like the hottest of fists clamping over his cock.

"Get up, mount your horse, and return to the estate. I will call on your father tomorrow."

Her eyes widened, and then her gaze dropped to his lips. A soft moan hissed from between her lips as if she reacted to the charged tension roiling from him.

"Payton, if you do not leave, I will hoist you onto the table, kiss you, tease and caress you as you desire…but I will not stop until I have you seated deep on my cock."

She gasped and lifted eyes that were darkened by desire and shock.

Christ.

A trotting horse broke the spell weaving around them. A good thing, for she had been close to climbing onto his lap and urging his lips to hers. Payton drew away from the temptation of Mikhail and looked for the intruder.

Lord Jensen broke through the small thicket.

Anger, quick and sharp, surged through her. She stood and took an involuntary step in his direction before faltering. *What is he doing at Sherring Cross?*

A pleased smile broke across his face when he recognized her. With his golden blond locks, gray eyes, and wide smile, Lord Jensen was accounted as one of the most affable, charming young gentlemen of the *haute monde*. His countenance quickly darkened with disapproval when he noticed Mikhail and the glasses and bottle on the stone table.

"Payton, I would speak with you," Lord Jensen said, his voice clipped and angry.

She flushed at his lack of manners. A quick glance at Mikhail showed an expression of boredom, all traces of sensuality buried.

"Lord Jensen, may I introduce you to Mr. Mikhail Konstantinovich."

Mikhail stood and nodded in acknowledgment, and embarrassment flushed through her when Lord Jensen ignored him.

"Gather your horse and come. I will ride with you back to the estate."

"You have no cause to be so rude, my lord," she snapped.

"And I have no patience with your defense of this…" He seemed to gather himself. "I traveled nonstop to reach Sherring Cross once I received your father's reply to my request. I saw you race away without an ounce of decorum upon my arrival. I lost precious minutes readying a horse to come after you."

She glared at him. What request had he sent her father? A hollow sensation formed in Payton's stomach. "I did not ask for your interference, and you have no cause to ride after me. You, my lord, are not my keeper."

Anger darkened Lord Jensen's mien, and he dismounted, striding to her swiftly. "Do you understand the precarious position you placed your reputation in with your reckless little racing adventure? As your—" He broke off, his eyes narrowing on her lips. "Has this bounder kissed you?"

Payton stiffened in outrage. "My lord, you have overstepped your bounds."

"I know how your lips appear when they have been well kissed, for I have tasted from them enough times to know," Lord Jensen growled, anger mottling his face.

Mikhail subtly tensed.

Her heart pounded, and mortification twisted in her. Lord Jensen's words made it appear as if she were a wanton who traded kisses with any man to pay attention to her.

"I…" Tears pricked behind her lids, and he reached for her.

"Do not touch her." Though spoken softly, Mikhail's words were infused with cold command, freezing Lord Jensen.

Payton did not wait to observe his reaction to Mikhail's order. "Excuse me," she snapped, and raced past Lord Jensen to her horse.

"Do not presume to tell me I cannot touch my fiancée," Lord Jensen hissed.

Payton stumbled. *Fiancée?*

Gripping the reins of her horse, she faced him, her heart thundering in her ears. He was here because her father sent for him.

No. Her father wouldn't. He had always been her ally in the war with her mother and aunt. She glanced at Mikhail. He stood with his feet braced apart, his hands thrust deep into his pockets his eyes remote and carefully masked.

Call on me. She mouthed the words, and tenderness pierced her when a slow smile curved his lips.

Mikhail strolled over, gripped her hips, and helped seat her on Aeton.

"Thank you," she whispered, and rode away ignoring Lord Jensen's shout for her to wait for his escort.

She prayed his presence did not mean what she feared, but somehow she knew it did, and the battle she had planned for independence seemed as if it had arrived far sooner than she anticipated.

Chapter Nine

Payton sequestered herself in her room for the rest of the afternoon. She had even declined to luncheon with the rest of the guests, furiously writing down all the reasons she wanted to choose her own husband. Her mother would ignore them, but her father would at least lend a listening ear. Or so she hoped.

Aunt Florence had barged into Payton's chamber earlier, a whirlwind of excitement, and informed her Lord Jensen St. John was in the smaller parlor. Knowledge of what awaited settled in her stomach like bad ale; he was the last man she wanted an audience with today.

A luncheon tray had been sent to her room, and she had kept him waiting while she ate. After much haranguing from her mother, Payton dressed in a simple lime green day gown, caught her hair in a loose chignon without the aid of a maid, and slipped her feet into walking slippers.

A mere hour later, she moved with determined steps to the parlor.

"I urge you to give him a fair hearing, my dear," her aunt

murmured.

Payton cast a glance down the dimly lit corridor, hoping she could stumble and sprain her ankle, saving her from the conversation about to happen. "Do you know what he wishes to speak of, Aunt?"

Aunt Florence clasped Payton's arm and gave her an encouraging smile. "I have some idea."

Denial surged inside Payton. It was Aunt Florence's shoulder she had cried on so piteously when he'd distanced himself without even a letter. Why had she expected her aunt to be loyal? "Aunt, I cannot—"

"Give him a chance, my dear. At least listen to what he has to say with an open heart. And know your father has already given his blessing."

With a gentle squeeze of her hand, Aunt Florence stepped back. Nervous energy coursed through Payton, and she took a calm breath, opened the door to the parlor, and sauntered in as if she had not a care in the world. A soft *snick* sounded, and she faltered. Her aunt had closed the door and left her alone with the dratted man.

Since being jilted she'd received several propositions, from amusing to really vulgar, with which she had dealt with cool aplomb. Yet to see Lord Jensen in the parlor waiting for her with an air of confident expectation had sweat breaking on her brow. "Lord Jensen, this is a charming surprise." The lie soured on her tongue, but she would be pleasant and ladylike, and would be as firm as possible in denying his request for reacquaintance without being abrasive. "Why have you requested an audience?"

"Payton—"

"Miss Peppiwell," she said with a tight smile.

"There was a time you allowed me more than simply calling you by your given name," he insinuated softly.

Her heart lurched. "And there was a time I thought

you a gentleman with honor who was worth according such liberties. Alas, we must learn to live with disappointment." *Three kisses.* And she was glad she had not allowed more despite his gentle persuasions.

A look of discomfort flashed across his face. "This is why I wish to speak with you so urgently."

He had the gall to pat a section of the sofa beside him.

She moved across the room and sat on the chaise farthest away from him. Annoyance shafted through her when he launched to his feet and rushed to her side, kneeling down, gripping her hands. *Good lord.*

"I admire you most ardently," Lord Jensen said with an earnestness that would have charmed her several months ago. "I have been foolish, Pay—Miss Peppiwell—and I beg your forgiveness. Nothing would make me happier than if you would consent to be my wife."

Lord Jensen did not admire her. How could he even think she would believe such a thing possible after his atrocious behavior?

Please do not let their ears be pressed to the door. Payton would not be able to endure the anger of her mother and her Aunt Florence at such an early hour. She stood and, with deliberate steps, she walked to the door and opened it.

Thank heavens.

After ensuring her aunt had not lingered in the hall, Payton returned to the parlor. She smiled gently and regretted it immediately. The look of anxiety in his eyes dispelled, when she had only smiled in hopes of lessening the sting of her rejection. "Please, my lord, stand."

He stood and sat beside her on the chaise, clasping her fingers. Payton withdrew her hand, uncaring that she might offend him.

She searched for polite words to decline his offer. "Your offer is indeed generous, and I thank you for making it, but

I cannot marry you. Please believe me when I say I take no pleasure in causing you discomfort."

"I love you, and from our many walks I believe you return my heartfelt affections."

She found him singularly lacking. "While I appreciate your sentiments and the courage it must have taken for you to declare yourself, I do not return your *heartfelt affections*."

"What?" He looked genuinely bewildered and hurt. "I love you, Payton."

She searched for the spark of interest, that sweet feeling of delight, and only felt regret for lost time and a possible friendship. "Forgive me for causing you pain. It is not my intention. But I hold no such affections for you, and I cannot marry you, Lord Jensen."

It seemed as if her words finally penetrated, because he froze, and the utter shock that filled his eyes had tension shifting through her.

"I do not think you understand," he said, lips tightening, all affable charm vanishing. "I am offering to make you my future viscountess, despite your lack of recommendations."

She stiffened, knowing what was about to come. The reminder of her supposed inferior circumstances. "I have given you my answer, my lord."

He puffed up like an angry bird. "Who do you think you are to reject me?"

Her palm itched to slap the look of condescending hauteur from his face. She rose and graced him with a polite smile. "Good day."

He rushed to her, grabbing her hands. He pressed a fervent kiss to her cheek, and she jerked from him. "Lord Jensen, please conduct yourself like a gentleman," she snapped, thoroughly angered by his persistence.

"I cannot stay away from you, Payton, I ache for you."

She narrowed her eyes in warning. "You are aching for a

slap, my lord, one I will not hesitate to give."

He placed his hands over his heart as if she had pierced him. "Why are you being so stubborn? You said yes to my offer last year, and we never called off our engagement."

The depth of rage that surged through Payton rendered her speechless for precious seconds.

Seconds he used to tug her closer. "Your father has already given me his blessing."

She yanked her hand away from him. "How dare you," she whispered.

"Payton, I —"

"Be silent!"

He flushed, and awareness of her anger seeped into his eyes. A look of regret and possibly shame chased his features, but nothing softened inside of her.

"You abandoned me, you ignored my letters asking for explanation. You do not get to come here and pretend that you did not act abominably. I will not be forced where my heart does not lay. My father giving you permission to court me is irrelevant."

"Is this about that blasted man you raced away with earlier? I made some inquiry, and the man is nobody, Payton. It is shocking that you rode with him without a chaperone and allowed him to kiss you."

"Please excuse me." She owed him no explanation, and she did not look back as she fled to the sanctuary of her chambers.

Several hours later, the door to the Rose Room swung open without a knock. Payton lifted her head in startled surprise. This was where she escaped to etch her drawings and to craft the stories. Hardly anyone ever intruded after Lady Calydon made it known the Rose Room was to be Payton's sanctuary whenever she visited.

Aunt Florence stood in the doorway looking flustered.

Concern curled through Payton, and she closed the book with her drawings. "Yes, Aunt?"

"You are needed in the smaller drawing room, my dear. Your parents await you."

"Mother and Father?"

"Yes."

She'd tried to speak with her father after leaving Lord Jensen, but her father had indicated he was busy and would call for her at his earliest convenience. Payton had wanted to speak with him alone.

An audience with her mother and father was never a good thing. It meant they were in perfect agreement with whichever torturous command they would soon inflict. She stood and tucked the leather-bound volume under her arm.

Could it be Lord Jensen had taken his asinine demands again to her father? Dear God, she hoped not. More than two hours had passed since she rejected him, and from the windows in her chambers she had witnessed him walking on the lawns with Lady Ophelia Clayton, and Payton had hoped he'd accepted her rejection. She moved rapidly to keep pace with her aunt and arrived at the smaller drawing room in short order. Payton paused and took a deep breath, steadying her nerves, and then entered behind her aunt.

Her father stood by the fireplace, his hands clasped behind him. He turned at the closing of the door, and Payton's heart jerked at his serious expression.

"You asked for me, Father?"

His gaze roamed over her, searchingly, but he did not speak. She glanced at her mother who sat stiffly on the chaise in the far left corner, her lips thinned with displeasure.

What is it?

She stepped farther into the room, while Aunt Florence went to sit beside her mother and clasped her hands.

Sudden fear jerked through Payton. "Are Phillipa and Phoebe well?"

"Your sisters are well," her father said, his voice neutral.

Relief pulsed through Payton, and a heavy sigh escaped her lips. "Thank heavens."

"You will marry Lord Jensen St. John within the fortnight."

Surely she misheard.

"I was compelled to ask His Grace for his assistance in obtaining a special license. You *will* marry the honorable Jensen St. John."

It was as she feared, and shock held her immobile. A dull roaring sounded in Payton's ear. "A special license?"

Her father waved toward the corner, and it was then she noticed the duke standing by the mantel, his face carefully blank.

"Yes," her father snapped, his face mottling.

She pressed her clasped fingers to her stomach, hoping to stop the churning nerves that would see her chucking up her light luncheon. "Forgive me, Father, I do not understand. I have no wish to marry Lord Jensen. He made an offer earlier, and I rejected it. I have expressly told Mother and Aunt Florence I am not—"

"It matters not what you wish," her father roared. "*I* have accepted his offer, and you will marry him or so help me God…"

The anger he vibrated with had Payton's stomach plummeting. What was wrong? He had always been her most avid supporter. "Father—"

"I allowed you too much freedom. I indulged you and Phillipa, and disgrace was almost brought to this family. If not for the honor of Lord Jensen, we would have been none the wiser of your behavior, young lady."

My behavior? Confusion rushed through her at the sob from her mother. What was going on? Nothing would induce her to marry the man who had treated her with such contempt, and Payton knew she had a fight on her hands. "Will someone please tell me what is happening? Mother is crying and, Father, you are speaking of matters of which I am ignorant." She did nothing to hide her exasperation, though she feared her anxiety bled into her demand, betraying the depth of her nervousness.

"Lord Jensen has informed us of the shocking encounter he had with you last season at Lady Graham's midnight soiree," Aunt Florence said softly.

The memory of the night scythed through Payton, and she visibly jerked, a blush staining her face.

"Good heavens," her mother cried, quite theatrically. "It is *true*."

The room went deathly quiet with the crackling fireplace the only sound. What could she say? He had kissed her, more than once, and she had returned his embraces. He had just proposed, and the excitement of helping her family attain what they had longed hoped for had swept her away.

"I believe this is where I exit," the duke said, his fathomless gaze piercing Payton. "This is a family matter best discussed in private. I will procure the license."

She clasped her hands to hide their shakiness. "Please, Your Grace, I beg you not to. I cannot marry —"

A growl slipped from her father, and he rose to his intimidating height. "You will marry the man you thoughtlessly gave your virtue to. The man who has sought to do right by you, and whom you have ignored every step of the way. He thought there was a child, Payton. Lord Jensen believed this was the reason we had rushed you off to the country...to hide the child you had created," her father ended on a near shout.

She blinked stupidly at her father. *A child?* Who had a

child? Clarity broke through her muddled mind with sharp precision. She stiffened, outrage pouring through her. "I assure you my virtue has not been compromised. Lord Jensen only kissed me!" Mortification burned through Payton, but she held her father's volatile glare.

He gave her an incredulous look. "Do not believe me to be a simpleton, daughter. I may have been neglectful in doing my duties since I have been in England, but no more."

Anger nearly choked her. "You cannot be serious. Lord Jensen and I…I…never…" Her entire face burned to be having such an intimate discussion with her father, and in the presence of Calydon. Why would Lord Jensen behave in such a despicable manner?

She moved closer to her father. "I swear to you, Father, on the night he proposed to me, he kissed me twice, very chastely I might add, *nothing* that would warrant a wedding."

"Why would Lord Jensen, the heir to the viscountcy, lie about—?"

"How do you know they were chaste kis—?"

Her parents broke off their simultaneous questions to glare at her.

"Lord Jensen would not lie." Her mother spoke first. "He is a gentleman. The son of a viscount. You must allow him to do the honorable thing and marry you."

Payton stared at her appalled. As if Lord Jensen's title elevated him above being despicable. "He is lying," she insisted. "I cannot fathom his reasons, but I assure you, Mother, I never acted in the manner he is insinuating."

Aunt Florence exhaled with relief and gave her a small encouraging smile.

Her father ignored all of that, clasped her shoulders, and peered down into her face, his eyes blazing with anger. "How did you know St. John's kisses were chaste, young lady?"

What?

"Father, this is utter madness." She wanted to throw her hands in the air and scream. She felt attacked from all sides, without a supporting face in the library.

"How?" he roared, and she jumped, pulling from his tightening grip.

Instinctively her gaze flicked to Calydon. A blush heated her face, and she saw awareness dawn in his eyes, then a pleased smiled curved his lips. Why was he pleased?

"Father…I…I am assuming, I am not sure of anything at this moment," she ended, ashamed to feel tears burning behind her lids. "I would appreciate it if you would lower your voice."

Her father advanced, and she retreated. Never would she have imagined this confrontation at being summoned. Why would Lord Jensen do this? According to his mother, Payton's possession of a sizeable dowry was her only recommendation, and it had not been good enough.

Acting on the instinct of flight, she rushed to the door.

"You will not leave this room until you have answered my questions to satisfaction," her father snapped. "Lord Jensen alluded he saw you riding alone with…with a horse breeder, and I had not believed my daughter could act with such wanton impropriety."

Her mother gasped and then swooned, quite dramatically.

"Mr. Konstantinovich is not a stable hand. He is His Grace's man of affairs and a friend. Yes, I rode out with him, but we were in view of the croquet party." Not quite true, but she could not bear to reveal any more. The entire situation was mortifying and heartbreaking.

"I am ashamed," her father said quietly, and she flinched.

"I have done nothing to bring you shame," Payton said hoarsely.

He held her gaze, and then nodded. Her mother sobbed quietly in the background, but Payton did not spare her a glance. It was her father she needed to convince. "Father, please believe me when I say—"

"No," he said. "I have spoken, and I have informed Lord Jensen he can make the announcement in the *Gazette* and the *Times*."

Betrayal scythed through Payton. "You would believe Lord Jensen over your own daughter?"

"Do not cast aspersions on the man wishing to marry you," her aunt gently berated.

Payton's throat burned. "I know this family desires to move amongst loftier circles. I never believed my father and mother would place their desires above my happiness."

Her mother gasped, but her father stood immovable.

"The reason I am consenting, Payton, is because you gave yourself to him. Phillipa acted in a similar reckless manner, and I did nothing. No more," he snapped coldly. "You will marry Lord Jensen, or I will disinherit you."

Without speaking she turned from the room and ran.

Chapter Ten

No, no, no, no!

Payton ran into the icy outdoors toward the stables. In her periphery she saw Lord Jensen rushing after her, and she hurried her steps. Her emotions were too volatile to face the lying wretch; she was liable to slap his face with all her strength, which would no doubt create a new wave of scandal, since several of Lady Calydon's guests were strolling on the front lawn and through Sherring Cross's famous gardens.

Averting her gaze from everyone, Payton did not halt until she reached the stables. The scent of worn leather and horses filled her nostrils, and she headed for another stallion, one that had already been fitted with reins and saddle, no doubt for one of the guests.

Without hesitation, she used the mounting block and seated herself astride, pulling the hem of her day gown to her knee in the most indecent fashion.

"Payton, my darling, please let me explain," Lord Jensen said, running to stand beside her.

Rage blasted through her. Her hands trembled, and she

fisted them on the reins, not wanting to betray the depth of emotions roiling through her. Payton prayed her face was filled with all the distaste she felt as she looked down on him. "You are despicable, and *nothing* will ever persuade me to wed you."

The concern and charm shifted, and anger flared in the gray depths of his eyes. "Your father has already given his blessing. And if you think to make this difficult, I promise I will *ruin* you. How many men do you think will want you after I have made it known I've had you? You think you know what it is to face ostracism? All London will speak of is that I took your virtue, and no man will offer for you, whether he be high or low born."

She gasped, shock pouring through her. "A few months ago all it took for you to shift your affections was a rumor of Lord Anthony and Connie's bastardy. Now you are so eager to marry me, even if I feel only contempt for you. Why? My dowry and inheritance?"

A grimace twisted his lips. "It is vulgar to speak of money so casually, but I suppose I cannot expect better." His eyes flicked to her exposed legs and lust heated his gaze. "We will be good together, Payton. Just give me a chance…give us a chance. Now get down so we can discuss this in a becoming manner," he ended patronizingly.

Smothering a very unladylike curse, she surged away.

He yelled her name, and she ignored him, bursting from the stables. Payton urged the horse she rode to almost breakneck speed. She had to get away. Thunder grumbled in the distance. The gloomy weather seemed to be in perfect tandem with her emotions. Lightning cut across the sky, followed by another blast of thunder. A squall brewed, but she would not return to the main house. She could not face more arguments or tearful pleading from her mother.

I cannot marry him.

She rode hard, blanking her mind from the emotions trying to swamp her. Without realizing it, she had directed the horse to the cabin where she had met Mikhail. She could see it in the distance, and she slowed the horse, bringing him to a canter until they broke through the clearing before the cottage. She swept from the horse and released his reins. It made no sense to tether him with the approaching storm. Nor did she care if he fled and left her there. The longer she was away from everyone the better.

Payton ran up the small cobbled steps and slammed into the cabin, a harsh sob tearing from her. How could her parents believe Lord Jensen over their own daughter? Or did they know he lied, but were willing to accept another noble gentleman into their lives at all cost? They had already doubled her dowry in an evident bid to buy a title.

She no longer held any love for Lord Jensen and could not imagine her life as his wife and viscountess. She tried to remember the wonderful times they had together in the past, hoping to recall the warm thoughts of affection she had felt during his courtship. The only feelings roused in her were the ones of emptiness she had endured when he had stopped calling for days, weeks, when the rumors of Lord Anthony and Connie's bastardy had roared through society. Payton had even written Lord Jensen and, to her undying embarrassment, her letters had been returned to her unopened with a scathing note from his mother.

Why would Lord Jensen now be so amiable to forming an attachment? It could only be her money, and such a motivation for marriage was wholly acceptable to society and her family. *But not to me… What about love and respect*?

Inevitability weighed down on her, and she pressed a hard fist to her stomach. *What am I to do?*

The door to the cottage was thrown open, and she barely stifled a scream. She breathed a soft sigh of relief when

Mikhail strolled in, his hair tousled by the winds, his white shirt clinging to his damp chest. He must have been right on her heels, and she had not noticed.

She took an involuntary step in his direction before grinding to a halt. "What are you doing here?"

"You rode away from the estate as if the devil were after you."

Her gaze flicked to his curious own, and the storm of emotions that had been gathering inside her grew in strength. "Were you the only one to follow me?"

He stepped farther into the cottage, dwarfing the small place with his presence. "As far as I could see."

A harsh sob tore from her chest, and she wanted to hurl herself into his arms but buried the impulse. The desire was reckless and more than foolhardy. Despite their illicit kiss and the feelings he roused in her, her father would never accept Mikhail's suit. Not when Lord Jensen had made his wishes so clear to a family only seeking greater elevation into the *haute monde*.

Lightning flashed across the sky, and seconds later, torrential rain gushed from the heavens, battering the roof of the cottage. The memory of their first meeting simmered through her, and the awareness of how alone they were seeped into the air. What she saw in his eyes was not calm and controlled.

"You should not be here, Mikhail." It could all be in her head, but his presence in the cottage was dangerous.

"What has happened to see you so distraught?"

She hesitated, and his gaze sharpened.

"You may confide in me, Payton. Are we not friends?"

Friends? Was that what their unusual relationship was... friendship? The need to unburden welled. "I..." She thrust her fingers into her chignon, tumbling the loose coil from its knot.

"You can trust me," he coaxed, his piercing gaze steady on her.

"My father has accepted the honorable Jensen St. John, heir to the Viscountcy of Kenilworth's, offer for my hand in marriage," she confessed softly.

Mikhail stiffened imperceptibly, a smooth mask descending over his face. "I see. And you object."

"Yes." Tears slipped down her cheeks, and she wiped at them with a furious swipe. *Do not cry*.

"Is your only objection because he is a lord?"

There was a curious undertone in his voice she could not decipher. But he seemed decidedly interested in her response.

"No! He is a liar who besmirched me to my parents…and even if he had not acted despicably I would have objected!"

Mikhail flinched. It was subtle but unmistakable. He stepped farther into the cottage, and she instinctively created more space between them. He noticed her shift, and a fleeting smile touched his lips, but he honored the distance.

"Tell me," Mikhail said, strolling to sit on the only table in the cottage, folding his arms across his chest, legs sprawled in a very ungentlemanly manner.

Something hot and uncomfortable hovered in the air between them, and she was too inexperienced to put a name to it. But whatever it was seethed in his eyes, and it reached from him like a caress, kissing against her skin, seducing her to relax her guard and unwind.

She briefly closed her eyes at her ridiculous fancy and walked to the small window of the cottage, leaning her forehead on the cool glass. "I wanted to marry Lord Jensen a few months ago. In fact, I was quite eager. But even before he cried off, the doubts had started. While we had a grand time at balls, and on our carriage rides, I had started to realize Lord Jensen did not care much for my accomplishments. When I tried to share my passion for crafting fairy tales, he smiled indulgently and informed me as a future viscountess I would not have to lower myself to do such works. Aunt Florence had encouraged me to keep silent about my writing, saying the *haute monde* would think me silly…that Lord Jensen would find my ambitions unbecoming. I am ashamed to say I repressed much of myself to secure a well-made match."

She pushed from the window and turned to Mikhail. "He *jilted* me. And I was hurt and angry. Hurt he would think so little of me, and of the wonderful persons Lord Anthony and Lady Constance are."

Payton balled her hands into tight fists. "He abandoned me without a word. He drifted away, stopped calling, and was not gentleman enough to face me to end our engagement. Against my aunt's advice, I visited his home, and I was not even admitted." Payton ended on a whisper, the humiliating memory twisting her stomach into knots.

The entire situation infuriated her. "I moved past his betrayal, society's derision, and I even started to feel relief. Happy I had escaped what might have possibly turned out to be a shallow union. And now he is once again pursuing me, and my family pretends he did not shred my heart because he is a *lord*. I will not wed a man who treated me with such little regard," she growled.

"Then do not marry him."

She paced, agitation battering her senses. "You do not understand, Mikhail. If my father says I must, what choice do I have?" She closed her eyes. "I will flee. I have been thinking to return to my grandmother in America. It will be a daunting journey to take by myself, but I fear I must escape my family's persistent pressure or crumble to their demands and join in an unhappy union."

His veiled gaze settled on her face. "What happened to prompt this command?"

She fought to control her emotions. It was silly of her to

feel betrayed. She had long accepted that Lord Jensen had no honor. She tried to swallow down the raw emotions rising in her throat. "He lied to my father. St. John has insisted he took my chastity when we were engaged. I never gave myself to him! It is convenient for my mother and aunt to believe it, for they will get their hearts' desire for me to be a viscountess. I will never marry into the *haute monde.*"

The sob she'd been valiantly holding on to broke free. *Oh God.*

Mikhail pushed from the table, and in two strides he was there drawing her to him. Strong arms closed around her, and she eagerly burrowed into the warmth and comfort in his reassuring embrace, slipping her hands around his waist and hugging him tight.

He froze, and she heard the thud of his heart against the side of her face pressed into his chest.

"I apologize," she whispered, dropping her hands from his waist. "I forgot your aversion to touch."

He cleared his throat. "Think nothing of it; I would welcome your embrace for a few moments if it would ease you."

The words wrapped around her heart, terrifying and intriguing, because she somehow knew he had never made the offer to another. A new type of warmth unfurled in her chest. She wanted to twine herself around Mikhail, burrow further into his heat until the uncertainty faded. But she could not. Though he offered, he braced himself stoically for her to accept, his eyes shadowing with unnamed but volatile emotions. She shifted in his arms and tilted her head to look at him fully.

His gaze was shuttered, and the tenseness had yet to ease from his frame.

"I am contented, thank you." Then a horrible thought occurred. What if he hated touching her as well, and because of her inexcusable tears he was forcing himself to hold her, to offer comfort? "Would you like me to step back?"

"No…I would be a foolish man to want to relinquish a beautiful lady from my arms."

Payton smothered a snort, and he chuckled, the sound dark and full of sensual promise.

"Do you want me to release you?" he asked, his voice low and rough.

Acute awareness of his hands resting against her back, the far-too-intimate nature of their embrace slithered through her. In his touch she felt strength and restraint. His closeness should have intimidated her and made her feel nervous, but he provided a curious sense of comfort. "No. I want you to hold me closer."

Surprise flared in his eyes, and then he masked it. The need to pierce his armor welled in Payton. She lifted her fingers to his lips. She touched him with a featherlight caress, fleeting and tentative, gliding her fingertip across his jaw.

He tensed, but he did not retreat, and Payton claimed a small victory in a war she did not understand. "I want you to kiss me."

His breathing fractured. "No."

She swallowed, and a blush climbed her face. Once again she was being very unladylike, all her aunt's deportment lessons forgotten. Before she could question him, he dropped his arms from her and stepped away.

"I can see the questions forming in your eyes. Do not doubt the strength of my desire for you, Payton," he said. "But I cannot accept the invitation in your eyes until I speak with your parents about courting you."

"You want to court me…for possible marriage?"

"Yes."

The reason Payton had been happy with the honorable Lord Jensen was because he'd made her feel safe in the uncertain and privileged world of the *haute monde*. She'd agreed to marry him before, knowing she would never taste the depth of passion her sister, Phillipa, had burned with when she'd spoken of Lord Anthony. Since meeting Mikhail, Payton had felt the potent rush of desire in a manner that was shocking, but was it enough to consent to courtship knowing her family's objection? Knowing how much she had been hurt before when she had dared?

His blue eyes darkened and blazed with need while he waited for her response.

She was stepping dangerously close to falling for a man she hardly knew. "I have tried harder to be more ladylike." He reached for her, and she held up a hand, halting him. "I…I feel things with you I have never felt with another…I actively think of *kissing* you. You do not have expectations of ridiculous ladylike behaviors, and you have afforded me the courtesy of being myself. I would like to get to know you more…but my father would *never* consent to you calling on me, especially now."

"Is that your only objection?"

"I…yes…maybe."

He raised an enquiring brow.

"I never thought I would agree to courtship again so soon." She had known Lord Jensen for several months, and his actions had still caught her off guard. "I do not want to be hurt, and I do not want to hurt you."

"I will not hurt you."

She snorted. "You cannot promise that, and I will not tolerate another gentleman abusing my feelings."

"Does this mean you will never open yourself again to a man?"

"No…I do eventually want a family."

"Pain is a part of life," he said, a dark undercurrent in his tone. "I will do everything in my power not to hurt you." A guarded look descended over his face. "I cannot promise I will succeed, but I will promise to never willfully cause you pain, and I will promise to give everything of me that I'm able to give. You will not have cause to regret forming an attachment with me, Payton."

Everything he was able to give? "Will you also allow me to touch you?" *Please say yes.*

He stiffened, and she moved close enough to him that the hem of her dress curled around his shoes.

"You said you will give me as much as you are able to of yourself. Do you mean you will not allow my touch?"

Shadows shifted in the depth of his eyes. "Yes."

Never? Questions hovered on the tip of her tongue, but his shuttered mien urged caution. She retreated, gathering her thoughts. She enjoyed being with him, and she was willing to explore the budding feelings sprouting to life. "I will warn you, if you hurt me in a fashion that is deliberate or could have been avoided, me bashing your head in with a poker will be the least of your troubles," she said lightly.

Amusement quirked his lip, and he prowled close, sleek and graceful, shortening the distance she'd assumed he wanted. "Does this mean you want to know me more, that you will give me a chance?"

"Oh yes." A flush shivered through her at her much too enthused response.

The amusement fled from his gaze, and the intensity that replaced it had her heart squeezing.

He cupped her cheeks with both hands, tilting her head up, using one of his thumbs to swipe across her lower lip in an erotic caress. "Do not be embarrassed. I possess a similar need to know all of your secrets. I hunger to know your passion, what you dream of, the food you love, what makes you angry, what makes you throw back your head and laugh without a care in the world, what makes your golden eyes darken with need, and what makes you moan in abandonment."

His assertions burned all her doubts to ash. It was more than foolhardy, for her parents would never allow her happiness with him. "Books," she whispered.

"What?"

She swayed even closer to him, her breasts brushing delicately against his damp shirt. "When I smell a new book and clasp the leather binding in my arms, I moan…in pure pleasure."

His low chuckle rolled through the cottage, heated and gravelly, the sound one of ridiculous temptation. Thick, hot tension swirled around them.

"I have more wealth than you believe."

Her eyes widened. She had not expected him to say that. "I have never speculated on your money; it does not matter to me."

"I know, but it will matter to your family. And I believe when I make my wealth and stature known, my courtship will be welcomed."

Pain stabbed at the very heart of her. No, it would not. Her family would see him as beneath their lofty expectations though they were of the same social standing. An association with Calydon would not make Mikhail's suit welcomed. He *worked*…and he was wonderfully ordinary. They would not see the honor in this man, his kindness, or the fact that he would treat her as an equal. Payton did not know how to explain that this moment they were sharing might well be the last, once he expressed his interest to her family.

They would do everything in their power to ensure nothing or anyone so unconnected foiled their grand expectations. The pressure to wed Lord Jensen would mount, and she would either crumble or flee. She understood enough of English laws to know she could not run away with Mikhail and marry him without permission. Not even to Scotland and the famous Gretna Green she had read so much about in her romantic novels. If only her twenty-first birthday was not almost a year away. Payton feared the only moment she could have him was *now*, and she wanted his kisses and to dwell in a moment that was simply for her.

"I desire you to kiss me, Mikhail." This was *her* choice. "I want to feel your lips against mine, and I need to savor your taste once more."

A breath hissed from between his teeth, and carnality shifted across his face and settled like a second skin. "You are dangerous," he murmured.

Pleasure pulsed through her. "It is kind of you to say so… but I assure you, I am quite ordinary."

"No other woman has ever made my cock harden and my heart pound with a simple request for a kiss."

Good heavens. Curiosity beat against decorum…and won. "What is your cock?"

"Hell!" His eyes darkened to the deepest shade of blue, and tension coiled his frame. "You must not touch me…no matter the temptation."

Her throat dried, and she nodded weakly.

In a lightning fast move, he tugged her to him, and she tumbled into his embrace. He slanted his lips over hers, drawing a moan of pure need from the depth of her being. His taste was flavored with a hint of brandy, chocolate…and shocking eroticism.

She stood on her toes, sinking further into his wild kiss, losing herself and blindly twining her fingers through the hair curling at the nape of his neck.

He froze, his teeth sinking into her lower lips, lashing her with sensuous pain.

She stilled, her heart jerking erratically. "It is hard not to touch you," she confessed brokenly. "You kiss me, and I lose a piece of myself, unable to remember my promise."

Mikhail cursed under his breath, pulled from her and with rough movements drew his shirt over his head. Payton's knees wobbled. His naked chest rippled and twisted with strength. He was wonderfully formed, and she wanted so desperately to glide her fingertips across the expanse of his chest. Without speaking he walked to the wall where a sharp peg jutted and looped his shirt over it, then he grabbed the narrow bed and pushed it under the peg.

Payton couldn't speak. Anticipation and nerves twisted inside of her in equal measure.

"Come here."

The stark lines of his face were heightened by desire, the curve of his lips hinted at domineering sensuality, and if she were honest, she was a bit intimidated by his intensity, yet she was pulled to his side by the need trembling between them, and the knowledge she may never get such an opportunity to taste passion with this man again, this man who was *her* choice.

Payton sat on the cot, her feet barely touching the stone floor, her heart a drumbeat in her ears. The rumble of the thunder and the lash of the rain on the roof of the cottage did nothing to soothe her aroused anxiety. "What now?" Her voice was husky with need and the apprehension she tried to hide.

He moved over and stood in front of her. "Scoot into the center of the bed, raise your arms above your head, and grip my shirt. Do not let go."

She gasped at the shocking arousal that surged through her veins, and without hesitation, a testament to the trust she placed in him, she complied. The feel of his linen shirt fisted in her hands was an anchor in the midst of the tearing desire shivering through her limbs.

He sat on the bed, and it creaked beneath his weight. "Do you trust me?"

"More than I would have imagined possible," she breathed.

A slow smile creased his lips, moving him from sensual predator to charming seducer. He lightly encircled her left ankle and pushed to bend her knee, so she sat with her leg drawn up, the sole of her foot flat on the sheets. Her breath hitched when he leaned across, his fathomless eyes holding hers captive, and repeated the action with her other leg.

His eyes flicked to her hands poised above her head, gripping his shirt, before lowering in a heated caress to where she leaned against the small headboard, her bent knees pulling her dress to her shins, her ankles on shocking display.

"Open your legs."

Her gaze flew to his at the rough command. The deep blue of his eyes glinted with wicked knowledge, and God help her, but Payton complied, parting her legs invitingly.

Approval flared in his eyes. He coasted his fingers up the top of her leg, pushing her dress farther up, letting his thumb drag along the sensitive inside of her left thigh.

She clutched his shirt even tighter as his devilish fingers continued to the apex of her thighs, a frustratingly teasing caress. Without releasing her from his stare, he nudged her legs wider. Need coiled low below her stomach, and a heated throb started at her core. Her eyes widened when he cupped her mons and pressed gently. Pleasure consumed her, shrouding every logical thought.

"Have you ever been touched here?"

A fission of need rippled through her body. "Never." She pushed the words past her throat. For some reason, when he'd told her to sit on the bed, she had expected kisses. This was wildly inappropriate and simply decadent, but she desperately wanted to hold on to the aching pleasure dampening her drawers. "Touch me," she moaned, unable to bear the anticipation.

He shifted even closer, and his scent wrapped around her. He pressed a fleeting kiss to her mouth, and she parted her lips and darted her tongue to glide against his, hoping to tempt him into a deeper taste.

Holding her gaze, he shifted her drawers and slid a finger through her curls, down to part her. She was achingly wet and embarrassed.

"Look at me."

As if she could look elsewhere.

"Do you want me to stop?"

No! "You wouldn't dare," she warned.

"You are beautiful in your need. Do not ever be embarrassed to welcome this passion between us."

She nodded. "I feel as if you are speaking too much, Mikhail."

He laughed softly, and she leaned forward and stole the air from his mouth. He paused for a fraction, then his tongue stroked past her lips to meet hers in a sensual duel. She whimpered into the kiss when with maddening delicacy, he stroked her wet core with firm pressure, alternating rimming her entrance and flicking against her nub of pleasure. Their kisses grew hungrier, and Payton sobbed against his lips, so intense was the fever burning away all sense of herself. She craved.

He caressed the straining nub at the apex of her thighs over and over. On a sob, she arched up, yearning for the hovering fulfillment.

She squirmed with the need for more, and when he would not comply, she pulled from the kiss, breathing heavily. "I swear if you do not end this torture, I will release your shirt and strangle—"

He pushed two fingers deep into her without warning, sliding through the wetness he had created.

"Mikhail!" Pleasure and erotic pain lashed at her, causing

her limbs to tremble.

"Shhh," he soothed, brushing her lips with light kisses. He held his fingers still, allowing her to adjust to the wonderful strangeness of them buried so deep.

The only window to the cottage rattled, and the coolest of breezes rushed inside, but it did nothing to lessen the fever of need beating in her blood. "Is there more?" she demanded hoarsely.

"Infinitely," he murmured, wicked carnality suffusing his features. He withdrew his fingers and thrust in deep and slow. Her hips jerked, she pulsed, shivering deliciously.

"You are so wet and responsive." He inhaled, and his obvious struggle for control delighted her.

"There is nothing I want more than to draw you underneath me and bury my cock deep."

Temptation rose in her. There was the strongest possibility she would never feel such bliss again. She waited for the guilt to surface at the idea of going to a husband impure. But it was thankfully absent. "Then make me yours."

"No, my sweet, not until you are mine."

She heard the possessive way he said *mine*, and her throat tightened. "Yes," she agreed, and he smiled.

"But I will have your taste until that time."

Her taste?

He withdrew from her, and she gasped as he pushed her day gown and chemisette indecently high. He bunched the material at her waist, gripped her knees, and widened her legs.

"You will be tempted to release my shirt…do not."

Excitement pulsed through her. She watched him with acute curiosity as he tugged off her drawers, lifting one foot and then the other to remove them. She felt wicked and wanton, free and bold, and she never wanted this encounter to end. He slid his hand underneath her bottom, gripped, and pulled her to the edge of the bed.

His shirt tautened, and she tightened her hold, looping the ends around her wrists. He stared at the intimate part of her, and mortification blushed her entire body. Then he dipped his head and kissed her there.

Sweet merciful heaven.

He ran his tongue over her wet core in a toe-curling swipe.

"Mikhail, please, surely this cannot be decent," she moaned when he repeated the motion before clamping his teeth over her knot of pleasure and sucked…hard.

Her back bowed, and she gripped the shirt so tightly, she was surprised it did not fly off the peg. Her breath came in shuddering gasps, and a sob rose in her throat when he added his fingers to the sweet torment of his lips.

She tried to scoot back on the bed, overwhelmed by the erotic heat cascading through her blood, but he gripped her hips and brought her even more firmly onto his tongue. All of Payton's thoughts burned to ashes under the devastating pleasure Mikhail's incredibly wicked tongue and fingers delivered.

She sobbed his name, undulated her hips, whispers and hoarse cries ripping from her throat. The exquisite sensations built steadily, overwhelming her senses. Without thought she released the grip on his shirt, lowered her hands, and frantically clasped his head. She didn't know if she wanted to push him away or pull him firmer against her core. The lascivious thought had more heat spreading through her body, beading the tips of her nipples into hard points. They stabbed against her chemisette, desperate for a touch.

She sank her fingers into the thick strands of his hair and gripped tight as uncontrolled shivers scythed through her. His decadent tongue took her to the brink of sanity.

He froze, his teeth clenched with gentle but sensuous precision over her knot of pleasure.

Oh God. I am so sorry.

His eyes lifted to her, and the darkness swirling in his gaze was more than arousal.

Holding his eyes, she eased her fingers from his hair to her side where she fisted the sheets.

He scraped his teeth over her nub, then nipped once, twice, before drawing his tongue over her soaked slit, and thrust his two fingers deep and hard.

Payton shattered. Pulsating waves of pleasure coursed through her, and she tumbled into blissful delight. Despite the ecstasy, a fist of discomfort gripped her heart.

Will you ever allow my touch, Mikhail?

Chapter Eleven

Ice had formed underneath Mikhail's skin at Payton's passion-filled touch. He noted the burn of dread was less, but his gut still clenched in acute discomfort. He grimaced at the flash of pain in her eyes, before she lowered her lids, hiding her emotions, including the wanton heat. He had made more strides with Payton than he had with anyone in years. Was it because he liked and admired her? He pooled the dress over her splayed thighs, gently drew the flowing material down to her ankle, and assisted her in sitting up. She had yet to meet his eyes, and regret curled through him. *If only.*

He sat on the bed and laced their fingers. How could he explain he loved touching her…loved feeling the softness of her skin, but that he had to be the one in control of every caress, whether illicit or simply playful? Would there ever be a time he could relax with her and share his shame? *Maybe…*

His heart jerked, hard and painful, and he ruthlessly controlled his breathing. This was the first time in years he'd ever had the thought to confess his private hell to someone. Not even his brothers or Calydon knew the full of it…for

Mikhail had never spoken of his entire experience under Madam Anya. He didn't even like to entertain fleeting thoughts of that deceptive bitch, not when he was with Payton.

He reached forward and placed a finger under her chin and applied the slightest of pressure. "Payton."

She lifted her eyes to his, a tiny wobbly smile on her face.

"I wanted you to touch me. You held my head to your heat and for a wild moment I did not want you to stop. That has never happened to me before."

A flush rose in her cheek, washing pink across her face in the most becoming manner. "But…then…you did want me to release you?"

"Yes."

Her wince was subtle, but he spotted it. Unable to resist, he leaned in and kissed her. The need in him to soothe and offer comfort another way gripped him in a tight vise. It was startling to admit how much her feelings mattered to him. The madness of it did not escape Mikhail. He had only made her acquaintance a mere three days past, and he was sliding too deep…too fast.

She parted her lips and returned his kiss shyly, as if she had not just been lifting her hips in passionate demand. Her breath, a delightful scent of berries, slid over his mouth in a silken caress, and yearning shot through his heart.

Touch me, do not touch me. The dual needs warred, and he gritted his teeth until they ached. "We must—" He stiffened and listened.

Her eyes searched his face. "What is it?"

Blasted hell. "There is someone at the door."

Her face paled, and she jerked to her feet, staring at the door as if it were an apparition. "I believe you are mistaken, there—"

Her words strangled as her name floated in on the wind, and the door rattled under the pounding of a fist and not the wind.

"Oh my heavens. It is my father!" she said with a horrified gasp.

"I surmised." Mikhail had lost his head. Never had he imagined someone else followed when she raced away from the estate. But he should have realized they would have organized a search party with the inclement weather. He was so wrapped up in everything about her, he had not been thinking.

With swift movements he dragged his shirt off the peg and drew it on. It was crumpled with a multitude of wrinkles. He pushed the bed back in its slot and straightened the sheets as best he could. Then he turned to Payton.

Christ.

Only am imbecile would miss the flush of passion that still made her skin rosy, and the heavy-lidded arousal, but her anxiety and obvious embarrassment was doing a damn good job of hiding it. Her lips were swollen and red, her hair loose around her in wild disarray. It would be impossible to hide what they had just been doing a few moments ago.

He strode toward the door.

"What are you doing?" She gasped, rushing over to him.

"I am opening the door."

"You cannot!" Her hands went to her hair frantically, and with deft movements she gathered the heavy mass and tried to coil in into some sort of knot atop her head. The end result looked ridiculous, but she was filled with too much anxiety for him to point it out.

"Ooh!" She clasped her cheeks. "I cannot believe this is happening. Why would my father follow me? I think we should ignore it; maybe they will search elsewhere," she said on a hopeful note.

Tenderness curled through Mikhail, and a fierce rush of protective urge swamped him. He would bear her touch even if it killed him, if only to offer comfort. "Come here," he said, drawing her into his arms.

She flung herself against him and slipped her hands around his waist.

Distaste sliced through him, burning and roiling through his blood, scorching him like a poison-tipped knife. He could feel the frantic beat of her heart vibrating through his body. With a ruthless will he'd not thought himself capable of, he tampered his revulsion and returned her embrace. "It will be well," he soothed, gently circling her back. "This is unexpected, but we can face it. We are attired as best we can. And it may only be your father outside." He hoped. The man may have formed a party to search for her.

She groaned into his chest. "I had not even thought that he might have company."

Hell.

"It is tempting to ignore them, but the other cottages are farther away, and the weather is fierce."

As if to prove his point the rafter shuddered under a blast of thunder.

"My father is out there in this squall, without shelter," she said softly.

Sweat beaded on his brows as the burn of her touch became cold, encasing him in ice. "Yes."

"I'm sorry," she said wretchedly. "I never intended for this to happen!"

"I am not sorry."

She worried her bottom lip. "They will expect us to marry. It is too soon."

"I know," he said softy.

"What if we are forced to marry and we end up not *liking* each other?"

"You speak of the impossible. I already like you, and my desire to know your mind and body will only grow. I will have no regrets."

"Neither will I," she said into the soft of his throat, and he flinched.

She dropped her hands and pulled away from him. "Oh, Mikhail, I have been thoughtless. Please forgive me."

He heard the unvoiced need in her voice to understand, but he ignored it. "Think nothing of it; I hardly felt your arms." *Liar*.

She searched his face, then squared her shoulders and gave a decided nod. "Open it," she said, obviously bracing herself.

He gave her an encouraging smile and went to the door. Rain blew into the room, and there was shuffling of feet before her father stomped his way into the room followed by Lord Jensen, Lord Prendergast, and Lord Davenport.

They all jerked to a halt when they spied Payton standing in the center of the room, her hands clasped at her middle.

The silence was painful. Mikhail was about to speak when Calydon strolled in, wet and disheveled, his face carefully neutral.

Now was not the time to reveal his status, though it was tempting. Mikhail shook his head imperceptibly and Calydon raised a cool brow before his eyes flicked to the slightly rumpled bed and then to the very mussed Payton.

"Father, I—"

"Be silent," her father roared and she jumped, acute embarrassment suffusing her lovely features.

Her father raised his hand and advanced, his intention clear to all present. The chill of violence that tore through Mikhail had him stepping forward and gripping the man's raised fist in a bone-crushing grip, jerking him away from her. The unexpected move had her father stumbling to face Mikhail.

A fist. Her father would take a fist to her. He would abuse such a beautiful spirit.

"Do not ever make the mistake of raising your hand in anger in her presence again," Mikhail snarled. "For I will destroy you."

Shock widened Mr. Peppiwell's eyes, then anger suffused his features. "How dare you!"

Mikhail jerked the man even closer. "I dare because Payton is all that is sweet and wonderful, and you thought to offer her violence over a situation you do not understand. I will release you, but think carefully on your actions going forward," he warned softly, not wanting anyone else to hear. "If you hurt her, I will *ruin* you. The name Peppiwell will be nothing but dirt when I am through. And I will reach out my arms of influence and protect her from the destruction you will suffer."

He let the promise show in his eyes, then dropped his hand and stepped back. Mikhail looked at Payton, and pride snapped through him. Instead of cowering, she stood straight with anger firing in her golden gaze.

Lord Jensen glared at her father and stepped forward. "Is that it? You allowed this…this bastard to defile your daughter with his mere presence and you—"

"That is enough, my lord!" Payton snapped, a hectic flush rising in her cheeks. "You will not cast aspersions on Mr. Konstantinovich simply because we sought shelter together from the storm."

Her father latched onto the explanation he had not sought earlier with obvious eagerness. "Is that what happened? The storm forced—"

"Do not be blind, Mr. Peppiwell," Lord Jensen growled, advancing in the cottage while the other lords discreetly looked away from the scene unfolding. Only Calydon moved farther inside and closed the door.

"Her lips are swollen, and her hair is a mess." Lord Jensen

turned to Payton, his face mottled with anger. "Did you allow this common stable hand to fuck you and plant his seed—?"

The leash on Mikhail's patience and civility shifted, icy anger settling low in his gut. In a swift and tempered move, he slammed a punishing fist into Lord Jensen's filthy mouth. The man crumpled.

"Oh goodness, Mikhail," Payton gasped, hurrying closer. Instead of coming to his side, she stooped to where the man had fallen.

"Do not touch him." The cold rage in Mikhail's voice had her flinching, and she lifted startled eyes to his. He was not sure what he saw in his face, but she retracted her hand and rose gracefully.

"I would only check to see if he breathed."

He throttled back his anger, for it would change nothing, and the only thing that mattered now was protecting her. "I assure you he lives," he said flatly.

"You have harmed a lord, sir, and assault charges will be brought against you," Lord Prendergast said with a glower.

For the first time Calydon stirred. "You are speaking to—"

"Do not," Mikhail ordered, understanding his cousin was about to reveal his identity. This was not how he wanted to inform Payton.

"Then I urge everyone to calm the hell down," Calydon snapped. "This situation calls for strict temperance from the urge to gossip and utter discreetness, not anger." He pierced Lord Prendergast and Lord Davenport with steely glares. "This meeting will not leave this cottage, gentlemen. Miss Peppiwell is a treasured sister, and I will not sit idle while rumor twists an unexpected and innocent encounter."

Lord Prendergast and Lord Davenport gave stiff nods. Her father visibly wilted in relief, and Payton looked to Mikhail, concern glowing in her eyes.

"Lord Jensen," her father began. "He has—"

"I will confer with him when he rouses," Mikhail said softly. When he was through, the man would understand he should never approach her again.

"No, I will speak with the young lord," her father insisted stiffly. "He was only overcome with anger because he and Payton are to wed. He is very honorable and level-headed, and any man would be out of sorts at the idea of his future bride alone with a man unknown to us."

The man would insist Payton marry Lord Jensen, despite her state of obvious compromise with Mikhail. Distaste filled him. Was social elevation so important to her family? Payton did not want to marry a man like Lord Jensen, and her father was willing to employ force. Mikhail would not step away. He wanted Payton for himself. The idea of a lifelong commitment so soon should have rattled him, but instead it felt right. He would eventually marry, why not to a young lady who roused all of his interests? "I will visit you at your earliest convenience, Mr. Peppiwell."

He stiffened and glared at Mikhail.

"There is no need, sir, my daughter's fiancé understands that nothing happened here," Mr. Peppiwell said stiffly, though wariness glowed in his eyes. "They are to marry two weeks from today."

"I will call on you tomorrow morning by nine," Mikhail said flatly. How quickly Mr. Peppiwell will change his song once Mikhail revealed who he was. At least he could rest assured Payton actually liked him and not his social status. *But will she want me once she discovers I'm a prince?*

I will never marry into the haute monde. Her passion-filled snarl spoken just mere minutes past echoed in his head. He gritted his teeth until they ached. It was her acute dislike and distrust of all lords that was prompting Mikhail now to speak with her father first. She'd already told him to withdraw all thoughts of courtship if he belonged to the *haute monde*. He would inform her father and secure his silence, and then woo Payton until he was certain she would not reject him because of his connection to the realms. Otherwise she would rebel or even flee. He should feel some unease at his thoughts, but he'd always been ruthless is pursuing what he wanted...and he wanted her.

Discomfort flashed across Payton's face, and she moved as if to speak and then hesitated. Something akin to fear or maybe doubt flashed in her eyes. Coldness settled in Mikhail's gut. Why had she hesitated?

Was she regretting their shared passion? Worse, what if she now doubted forming an attachment because he could not bear her touch? He'd seen the pain in her eyes when he'd pulled from her touch. His chest throbbed with an unknown ache. Before he could do or say anything foolish, he turned and walked from the cottage into the lashing rain and tried to reason logically around the hollow sensation forming in his gut.

Chapter Twelve

"Mr. Peppiwell departed for London at the crack of dawn."

Mikhail grunted at the amusement in Sebastian's tone. He weaved and bobbed, slamming a fist in Mikhail's side. He could have dodged the punch, but instead he moved into the attack, welcoming the bite of pain. Rotating his shoulders, he sidestepped another precise and well-timed jab. They had been sparring for almost an hour, and sweat drenched Mikhail's skin, his muscles burned, and the reason for sparring at such an ungodly hour was sleeping soundly above him.

After being informed by the housekeeper that Mr. Peppiwell had left for London with a message to return in two days, Mikhail had mercilessly resisted the urge to climb the stairs and sneak into Payton's chamber. He wanted to know how she fared. The need had been powerful enough so that he had climbed the stairs and had paused on the final steps, battling the desire. A few guests had been walking along the corridor and had given him curious stares filled with rabid speculation. He'd cursed and retreated and instead dragged his cousin from his duchess with a growl to meet him in the fighting room.

He needed the distraction or he would likely do something stupid like whisk her away to the cottage and make love to her for days. Or worse, inform her of his titles before securing support and watch her turn from him. For the long night he had been restless, the taste and scent of Payton alive on his tongue, and the fear he may never be able to bear her touch rioting in his mind. He'd also known she would be facing censure from her parents and had wanted to be a buffer.

Then the very man whom Mikhail needed to outline his plans had departed at light. What was the man thinking? With a disgusted snarl, Mikhail marched from the mat and tugged the towel from the peg, raking it across his skin.

"You are going to marry her." A flat statement from Sebastian, but Mikhail heard the pleasure in his tone.

"Yes."

"Because you compromised her?"

"I wanted to court her and explore the feelings brewing for her before I lost my head and allowed us to be compromised." With a sigh he threw the towel against the rack, and then faced his cousin. "Wipe the pleasure from your eyes," Mikhail snarled. "She still does not know who I am, and may very well refuse my offer once she knows."

Calydon smiled. "Payton will not refuse your hand. Passion is a powerful motivator, and it will grow into deep affections."

Mikhail arched a brow.

"From what I gathered, she has only allowed Lord Jensen *chaste* kisses and that when she knew the man for months. Yet in a matter of days she has given you her virtue."

He stiffened. "Hold your tongue. She is untouched."

Skepticism suffused the duke's face. "I am not the only one to notice the rumpled bed and Payton's flushed appearance."

Mikhail growled, raking fingers through his damn hair as

he stalked to the window. He grabbed the ledge and pushed it open, appreciating the cold air filling his lungs. "I was reckless and could have damaged her reputation. The very scandal I so detest could now be circling her heels because I was unable to keep my head." He scrubbed a hand over his face, and he swore he could still smell the heady and decadent fragrance of her passion on his fingers. She had been so alluring and responsive. The wonder of her had been like his first brush with intimacy. It had been so long since he'd allowed himself to drown in his lover's moan and taste; everything had been so *new*.

Calydon walked to stand beside him. "You will not have to worry of gossips. The other lords will be discreet. They value the connection we have too much. And when it is made known you are Prince Alexander and the Duke of Avondale all hints of indiscretions will be forgiven."

The fickleness of society.

"I must travel to London and Kent," Mikhail said. "I will see my solicitors and attorneys. Open the houses and ensure the estates are aware of my arrival. They've had no notice I am in England, and it will take weeks to have everything sorted."

"You are revealing yourself?"

"I must…for Payton." *I will simply endure the scandal of my past when it rears its inevitable head much sooner than I would have wanted.*

"You sound uncertain."

Mikhail grimaced and took the cup of tea Sebastian held out. A maid had rolled in a tea tray some time ago, no doubt at the duchess's order.

"I will travel to London and speak with Mr. Peppiwell and council him to keep my confidence until I choose to reveal my status to Payton. I want the man to know who I am so he can stop pressuring her to marry Lord Jensen. I do not want to inform Payton of my titles yet. Her disgust with high society is deep, and my titles will not endear her to me. I need the opportunity to woo her, to make her fall in love with me, so she will not reject my offer once she knows. Without his support the man will not allow me a mile near her."

He sipped the tea, welcoming the warmth traveling to his gut.

"I know how much you value your solitude, but you are making the right decision," the duke said. "It is a bit underhanded, but I understand why you need more time with her."

Mikhail did not reply. He was taking a gamble, and he had realized hours past, the outcome was crucial to him, but deep in his gut, the knowledge hovered that he may have very well lost her already. The cards were stacked against him because of his titles. How much more would they slide against him when months, then years passed, and she realized he would never allow them to be too intimate?

The past two days had been a whirlwind of disaster.

"Payton, what were you thinking?" Her sister Phillipa said with a gentle scold.

Payton shrugged, unable to speak from the knot forming in her throat. Her sister had stopped at Sherring Cross last evening with Lord Anthony on their way to London. She had received Payton's letter and, instead of responding, Phillipa thought delaying their arrival in London for a brief side trip to the duke's home to view the man Payton was apparently falling for was a worthwhile detour.

Phillipa had heard all sorts of sordid details from their hysterical mother. Payton groaned just remembering the entire encounter. Mikhail had left the cottage, and she had wanted to rush after him, but for the first time in months, propriety had reared its head. Then Lord Jensen had groaned and stumbled to his feet, withdrawing a handkerchief from his top pocket to press against his bleeding nose, blustering about summoning his father and the magistrate. The wait for the rain to lessen had been the most painful hour of her life. Calydon had left the cottage as well, and she had suffered through Lord Jensen's blusters and assurances he would still wed her, a thing her father had been happy to hear.

Dealing with her mother's hysteria about how ruined they were had lasted until the wee hours of the morning.

"Payton, you are crying."

She groaned and swiped at her cheeks. "I am more unsettled than I realized." This was the first chance she and Phillipa had gotten to speak in private since her arrival. She had spent a couple hours with Jocelyn and the twins, and an inordinate amount of time soothing their frazzled mother.

Phillipa came over and rested a hand lightly on her shoulder. Payton met her gaze in the vanity mirror.

Phillipa's light golden eyes glowed with concern and curiosity. "Are you not feeling up to tonight's ball?"

Payton sighed. "No, but Mother will never forgive me, and I cannot endure another round of hysteria. The husband of Lady Davenport, the hostess, was at the cottage, and for some blasted reason Aunt Florence wants to test her knowledge."

And father has not yet returned from London. Not that he wouldn't firmly side with her mother and aunt. But he had always been the voice of reason, and she needed to speak with him. He had to consider Mikhail's suit.

"It is to get ahead of the possible scandal," Phillipa said with a grimace. "It is the way with society. Aunt Florence must see what Lady Davenport knows and deflect any whisper, with all the social power and grace she wields as the Countess of Merryweather. I know you may not want to hear this, but it is best you attend and do not seem to be hiding."

"I had not thought to hide."

Phillipa squeezed her shoulders gently in reassurance. "You look beautiful."

Payton nodded, flicking a glance at her reflection. Her hair was tightly bound without a strand out of place; a plait wrapped her head like a coronet. Strings of tiny pearls also dotted the roped plait, a perfect complement to the strands at her throat. She had also selected one of her more daring dresses, a sapphire-colored gown, with ruffled sleeves and a slightly scandalous neckline. She had wanted to feel beautiful tonight…in the event she saw Mikhail. Her breath audibly hitched, and a flush rose in her cheeks.

"Are you thinking of him?"

She lifted startled eyes to Phillipa.

"You are blushing, Payton," Phillipa said with a light laugh, moving to sit on the chair beside the small vanity. "Did you…" She took a deep breath and continued, "Did you allow him to make love with you?"

Heat flooded her face at the question. "No, but I wanted him to."

"Payton!" her sister gasped. "Then I am glad father arrived in time and saved you from being foolhardy."

"Do not lecture me, Phillipa. Not when I hold knowledge of all you had done with Lord Anthony *before* marriage."

It was her sister's turn to blush the color of her fiery red hair.

"Our situations are different," she muttered. "Anthony was determined to marry me."

So is Mikhail. Payton nodded, a mash of hope and despair roiling inside her. "When you gifted Anthony with your virtue, did you love him?"

Phillipa smiled gently. "I did…but I had not realized it. Do you love your Mr. Konstantinovich?"

Payton stood and walked to the bed, lifting her gloves and slipping them on. "I do not know. I thought I had loved Lord Jensen, and I wanted to marry him, yet the feelings I had for him were merely pleasant. After only a few days of acquaintance, the feelings Mikhail rouses in me are so intense, they sometimes make me question myself. I hunger to know him, and I yearn for his kisses. Is this love? The only thing I know for certain is I have never felt such passion for another."

Phillipa walked to her and clasped her hands. "It may not be love now, but it sounds like you are well on your way."

"Lord Jensen is distressingly persistent, and mother and father are insisting that I wed him in a few weeks, instead of allowing a drawn-out engagement."

"I know," Phillipa said soothingly. "They are hoping a wedding will quash the potential for scandal...and they do not want Lord Jensen to change his mind again."

Payton got to the heart of what had been keeping her awake. "Mikhail wants to marry me."

Surprise, then delight, lighted Phillipa's features. "That is wonderful, I—"

"I blurted it to Mother in frustration, and she slapped me," Payton choked.

Anger flashed in Phillipa's eyes. She, too, had felt the brunt of their mother's anger and disappointment when she had dared to stand firm and insisted she would marry Lord Anthony despite his bastardy.

"I will speak with Father," Phillipa promised.

"Thank you," Payton whispered. "Mother already spoke to him, and he will only consent to me marrying Lord Jensen. I will not, Phillipa. I would prefer to risk sailing back to America."

"Wipe the anxiety from your eyes. Attend Lady Davenport's ball and have a grand time. I will speak with father when he returns in the morning, and you will promise not to act rashly."

"I promise," Payton said.

"Do you want me to come with you?"

"No, you are weary from your journey, and you seem tired."

A radiant smile pulsed from her sister. "I am exhausted."

"I never thought you would be so happy at the notion."

"Oh, Payton, I am with child."

"Good heavens." Payton drew her into a hug, laughing. "Congratulations. I am so thrilled for you and Anthony."

"It has only recently been confirmed, and we are keeping it to ourselves a bit longer, but I fear I cannot keep secrets from you."

A sweet feeling of joy curled through Payton. "Thank you for taking me into your confidence."

They exited the room together, and for the first time in hours a sense of peace washed Payton's senses.

The possibility had existed that Lady Davenport might have been made aware of Payton's seclusion in the cottage with Mikhail. After handing over her coat and strolling inside the small ballroom with an affected serene countenance, it only took a few seconds for Payton to realize *everyone* knew.

She descended the wide marble stairs to the ballroom floor, and she felt the weight of the guests' glares upon her. It could be her imagination, but the hollow sensation forming in her stomach reminded her of the times she had braved society after being jilted. Lifting her chin, she scanned the massive ballroom, looking for a friendly face. Dozens of eyes settled on her, some only indulging in a cursory glance, others from gentlemen in a lascivious and leering manner, and some outright rude as some young ladies giggled behind their fans, obviously discussing her.

"Why is everyone staring at us?" her mother fretted, none too softly.

A murmur rippled through the crowd, and people who had not been aware now directed their attention to Payton and her mother.

Payton's shoulder blades prickled with uncertainty under their rabid scrutiny. She felt like such an outsider, and it took everything in her not to turn around and escape up the stairs.

"Please excuse me, Mother, Aunt Florence."

A hand gripped her elbow and Payton paused.

"Remember, Lord Jensen will be in attendance tonight, and you are to save two dance spots for him," her mother whispered somewhat conspiratorially and with evident excitement.

Payton spied Lady Victoria and, with a smile, walked toward her without answering her mother. It felt good to see a friendly face that was not family. Lady Victoria was surrounded by a bevy of suitors, and Payton wondered if she should intrude.

"Blood will always tell. Can we really blame her for dallying with a horse breeder?"

She almost stumbled as the too loud whisper reached her ear. Payton glanced to her left at the huddle of females staring at her, their fans to their faces, gossiping.

Jilted. She heard the whisper from her right, and she flinched, unable to contain her reaction to the dreaded phrase. The word itself had become a weapon. Young ladies and lords alike had whispered it conveniently like a mantra whenever she drew close. She had hurt so horribly then. Lord Jensen had been the one to act with dishonor, but he had not borne any of the scorn. After a few weeks the need to scream had faded, and she'd become blessedly numb.

She turned left, intending to escape to the terrace when

another sly whisper reached her ear.

Ruined.

They were making no effort to be discreet.

A horse breeder.

She faltered and closed her eyes.

Lord Jensen still offered for her, after she lay with that horse breeder. He must be desperate to fill his coffers.

Bile rose in her throat.

What is the name of her horse breeder?

A Mr. Konstantinovich.

He sounds foreign.

What did you expect? No English gentleman of good breeding would willingly consort with the likes of her.

Lady Prendergast was right…blood will always tell, and it seems fitting for a commoner to lay with a horse breeder. It is terrible that poor Lord Jensen feels he must wed her.

The crush of the room almost stifled her.

Why was her ilk invited?

Her family shamelessly importunes upon the kindness of the Duke and Duchess of Calydon.

The curious side glances made Payton want to scream. Without looking to see who spoke, she pushed through the packed ballroom, her throat tight and burning.

"Some say he is a cousin to Calydon;" a closely whispered voice snagged her attention. She glanced at the speaker and identified Lady Prendergast.

"Everyone is agog to meet the new Duke of Avondale. I heard from the most reliable source that the town house at Berkeley Square is being opened."

"I have also heard he is alarmingly wealthy."

"He is a prince; embarrassing wealth is to be expected. He is Prince Alexander Dashkova, I'm told."

A sudden hush settled over the throng. She was jostled and pushed, but she moved against the tide, wanting to escape.

"The Duke and Duchess of Calydon, and Mr. Mikhail Konstantinovich."

It was as if the assembly gasped in unison, no doubt titillated that the very horse breeder they were discussing would appear. Of course no one would dare give him the cut direct, for he had arrived with the powerful Duke of Calydon.

She did not linger, nor did she turn to view them as they descended the ballroom steps. Payton escaped to the gallery that overlooked the ballroom and took a deep cleansing breath. Tonight felt especially painful, and Payton had never felt so wretchedly alone. She wished she'd not agreed to attend. She spied her aunt in the sitting room on the chaise lounge near the refreshment table speaking with Lady Davenport and several other society matriarchs. Aunt Florence was smiling and nodding, looking decidedly pleased.

Had they noticed Mikhail? Or were they pretending they did not know him?

Chatter mingled with muted laughter. Dozens of chandeliers created a dazzling display of light, women laughed and twirled, giggling behind their fans, a few even rudely pointing at some unsuspecting young lady, believing they were being discreet. Payton would prefer to leave everyone she had formed a connection with in England and escape back to America, before she would ever marry Lord Jensen and trap herself with such vicious harpies she would be forced to be polite to as his viscountess.

The hairs on the back of her neck lifted.

"You do not look happy to be here," a too-close voice whispered. How had he found her?

Temptation walked into her sanctuary in the form of Mikhail. Payton gasped at the picture he presented, dressed in so casually an elegant manner, in stark black-and-white. He was garbed in an expertly tailored black jacket and trousers. Only his crisp white cravat, waistcoat, and a white pleated shirt lightened the overall impression of darkness. His black hair was perfectly groomed, and the raw brilliance of his male beauty had her heart stuttering.

Without hesitation she gripped the lapel of his jacket and pressed her forehead to his chest, relief crashing into her. She buried her nose in his shirt, and his scent invaded her senses, rich and masculine.

"You are trembling, Payton," he said softly, his strong arms wrapping around her.

She had no thought for propriety or to worry someone else might intrude upon the sanctuary of the gallery. She was only happy he was present, a calm anchor in the midst of thundering pain and emotions their cruel words had elicited. His warm embrace was also a wonderful haven from the pounding demands she had faced recently. Everything faded, and she sank more into the security of his arms. "Where have you been?"

Gently he stroked her back and shoulders. "I traveled to London to see my solicitors," Mikhail said gruffly. "I had urgent business there. I tried to call on you, but you were abed. I left a note explaining my departure."

She had been up for hours dealing with her mother's hysteria and had been beyond exhausted, but she'd received no note. Anger, quick and powerful, cut through her. It was horrible they would go as far as to screen her letters.

"I gathered my note was not delivered to you." The wry humor in his tone had a fleeting smile touching her lips.

She nodded, her racing heart calmed, and gradually her tension flowed away. "I saved all my dances for you."

He stiffened, and she lifted her head from his chest.

His eyes blazed with hunger. "I feared you would no longer want to marry me."

"I have always been the dutiful daughter and Phillipa the rebellious one," Payton said with a small smile. "But in this I will not bow to their dictates."

A warm sensual smile curved his lips. "I will call on you tomorrow."

"You will be met with staunch resistance."

He exuded confidence. "Yet I will prevail."

"And I will be glad."

Shadows darkened his eyes. "There are things you do not know about me, that I must tell you."

"I do like secrets," she said softly. "But I can see yours have caused you pain. I will be here when you are ready to unburden."

His eyebrow arched in evident surprise. "I thought you would have insisted on traversing through my history."

She tipped onto her toes and brushed her lips across his in the lightest caress. "I, too, have secrets, and I promise you I will not divulge them after a mere five days of acquaintance," she said teasingly.

He pulled her even closer to him, holding her face in his hand. Then he dipped his head. The first soft touch of his lips to hers was a question, not a demand, and she responded with a moan of surrender. He slid one of his hands down her neck, resting his thumb against the beat of her pulse, and deepened their kiss.

He pulled his lips from hers. "I am embarrassingly wealthy."

"How droll," she teased, uncaring of his income. She prayed he did not believe it mattered to her.

"Hmm." He pressed another kiss to her lips. "My grandmother left me the majority of her wealth, and I have tripled it over the years. I rival Calydon's holdings."

Shock sliced through her. Calydon's dukedom was one of the richest in the realm.

"I do not think your assertions are possible."

Mikhail's eyes remained guarded. "They are."

"I do not care," she said. "I will worry less when my father disinherits me if I run away with you. But it is a wonder with such wealth, you are not able to purchase a title."

"I may have several hidden somewhere I can pull out for you," he said with humor, and something undecipherable glittered in his gaze.

Payton chuckled. A shadow shifted in his eyes, and she hesitated. Concern curled through her. What was he saying? "Are you titled?" she asked with a burst of nervous laughter.

"It is abhorrent you say the words with such dread. A title does not define a man."

"But it defines the world he lives in," she snapped, her heart thundering.

A soft laugh floated on the air, and footsteps drew close to where they stood in the shadows. She pressed a quick but hard kiss on his lips. "I must go before my aunt and mother descend on us."

Then she withdrew and entered the crush of the ballroom. It took Payton a few seconds to realize how rattled she was. The shadows in Mikhail's eyes troubled her. Could it be that he was titled? The possibility of it was too much to contemplate. What would a nobleman be doing working in the Calydon stables?

"Payton!" Her aunt's sharp but low call tried to pull her from her furious thoughts.

Mikhail had never said he worked in the stables. But he'd said he worked for Calydon as his advisor. From her experience, a lord would not be working. Then she recalled the tempered sense of power and grace that seemed to emanate from him so effortlessly, his confidence in the face of confronting her father and Lord Jensen in the cottage, his assurance her parents would accept him.

Uncertainty clawed at her stomach, and she wanted to return to the gallery and question him.

A possessive hand settled on her elbow. She lurched around to spy Lord Jensen, his mother, and Aunt Florence.

"Miss Peppiwell, you remember my mother, the Viscountess of Kenilworth," he said with a toadying and self-satisfied smile.

Payton pulled from him, none too subtly, and he narrowed his gaze in warning.

She allowed a smile to grace her lips and dipped into a curtsy. "Lady Kenilworth."

The viscountess barely nodded, gray eyes a replica of her son's, shooting distaste. "The execution of your curtsy was decidedly inelegant and shallow," she said, and Payton's palm itched to slap the smugness from her face.

"I believe this waltz was promised to me, Miss Peppiwell," Lord Jensen said, holding out his arm.

No, it was not. She could not suffer the thought of dancing with the lying arse. Denial hovered on her lips.

"This dance is mine," Mikhail's voice drawled from behind her. He looked to the viscountess and Lord Jensen, and greeted them with a small smile.

His veiled gaze settled on her aunt. "Lady Merryweather." Mikhail was chillingly polite, and arrogance was evident in every line of his bearing.

An awkward silence fell and spread.

"I did promise you all of my dances," Payton murmured, ignoring the shocked gasp of those close enough to hear.

Placing her hand on his arm, she strolled with serene grace to the ballroom floor.

It is the horse breeder, a voice close by hissed.

She felt as if his tall frame drew every female eye in the room.

How shocking, another thrilled, *are you sure?*

He is very handsome; I can see what tempted her scandalous behavior.

Murmurs rose from the people inside the ballroom, and Payton fought the blush heating her cheeks. There was nothing but amusement dancing in Mikhail's eyes.

Payton lowered her gaze, a smile pulling at her lips. "I feel as if the eyes of the entire *haute monde* are upon us." And the feeling increased, knotting her stomach with anxiety, for she knew how fast and vicious whatever gossips they bred tonight would spread.

"Then let them watch. Every man here envies my arms, for you are within them."

She chuckled. The waltz started, and Payton soared with Mikhail. She buried the fear that he might belong to the world she deplored, basking in the strength and assurance of being in his arms, baring all emotions she felt in her eyes, trusting him to be her wall if she crumbled.

"Would you like to leave?"

"No."

Something unfathomable shifted in his eyes. "I do not like that you are subjected to gossip. I promise you to change it."

She assessed the power rolling from him. *Oh God, please do not be a lord.* "The only whispers I can hear are the sighs of envy from all the young ladies. You are shockingly handsome," she teased.

His lips twitched, then he sobered. "Payton, I—"

Her heart lurched. "Yes?"

"Meet me tomorrow in our cottage."

"Yes." Reckless. Bold. But she did not care.

"Promise to hear me out."

Oh, are you a baron, a viscount? She wanted to ask the questions but held them in. They exchanged no words, and the intensity of his unwavering stare as he twirled with her was a comfort, a protective blanket from the malicious glares she could feel prickling along her skin. Questions hovered on her lips and in her heart, and she ruthlessly buried them and basked in the moment, for she could truly not tolerate the idea that the man she was falling hopelessly in love with may forever be taken from her grasp if he proved to be a lord.

No. She would enjoy this moment and then face her doubts in the light of day.

Chapter Thirteen

A procession of carriages and coaches drew into the Calydons' driveway. Cossack outriders flanked the procession, two to the front and two to the rear.

What is happening?

Payton closed the volume of the *Grimm's Fairy Tale*, the story of the *Elves and the Shoemaker* she had been reading, and strolled to the windows. She frowned as one of the most richly dressed women she had ever seen was helped down from a large and elegantly designed carriage pulled by Arabian horses. She was slender and graceful with her golden hair piled high in a riot of fashionable curls. *Oh, she is a beauty*.

Payton frowned as Vladimir appeared and bowed deeply over the woman's hand.

It was then she noted the duchess waiting at the doorstep, a frown on her lovely face. The procession moved toward the duchess, and Payton wished she were able to hear the conversation. The women greeted each other with curtsies, and the frown melted from Lady Calydon's face as she laughed at something the ravishing woman said.

Payton shifted her gaze to the entourage following the woman and the very handsome blond man at her side. With an inward shrug she dismissed their presence and settled in a chair by the fire and opened the book. She'd come to a point in the story she was crafting for the children where she was frustratingly unsure of how to proceed. Should she allow the princess to choose the royal guard or the prince himself? Both had journeyed together over marshlands and battled dragons and trolls to save the maiden only to find she'd already outwitted the gargoyles holding her captive.

The door to the smaller parlor was flung open, and Aunt Florence rushed in, distracting Payton from the unknown guest and her readings. Anxiety sliced through her, and she stood. She dropped the book on the chair, folded her arms, bracing for the fight. "I will not walk with Lord Jensen," she snapped. The persistent man had already demanded her company twice since morning, and she had refused. Of course he would now try to secure her family's support.

Her father had returned and was in the smaller library with her mother. They were probably discussing how to badger her into marrying Lord Jensen. She was also sure her mother was informing Father of her scandalous behavior in dancing with the "horse breeder" at last night's ball. She'd anticipated her father's roar of anger, so the silence was maddening.

Aunt Florence clasped her hands in front of her. "Your father has asked Lord Jensen to depart Sherring Cross and to no longer approach him for your hand."

Confusion and joy rushed through Payton in equal measure. "Oh, thank heavens." She made to rush past her aunt, but she halted Payton.

Her aunt beamed. "Give your father some time. Your mother is insisting on speaking with Pr—Mr. Konstantinovich, and your father has requested an audience to soothe her."

Payton frowned. "What?"

"It seems Mr. Konstantinovich saw your father in London and asked permission to court you. Approval was given."

She remembered Mikhail's confidence last night. Why had he not mentioned he'd seen her father? Was that what he wanted to speak with her about at the cottage today? But what was most amazing was her father's capitulation. He even sent away Lord Jensen. Sudden trepidation sliced through Payton, and dreadful knowledge hovered. "Father and Mother have no objections to Mr. Konstantinovich courting me?"

Aunt Florence hesitated. "Your father will speak with you, my dear."

Before she could demand more clarification, the door was flung open, and the beautiful woman from outside swept in, the unknown man and Vladimir at her side.

"Is that her?" the woman demanded scathingly with a pointed glare aimed at Payton.

"Princess Tatiana," Vladimir started soothingly. "It is best we wait until the prince is available. He will not take kindly to you upsetting the girl, and it was not my intention for you to force a confrontation."

What prince? And why were they speaking of her as if she were not present? Payton dismissed them and moved to walk out of the parlor. She would head to the cottage and wait for Mikhail. Why had he not informed her of his visit to her father?

"I have not finished speaking with you," the woman snapped, stepping rudely into Payton's path, looking down her thin but elegant nose with disdain.

Payton stiffened. "I beg your pardon. I was not aware you'd addressed me."

The princess's lips parted in a contemptuous sneer. "She is an American." She shot an accusing stare at Vladimir. "You had me worried for naught. He would not dare to think to align himself with someone so unworthy of his family's name.

I am sure you misunderstood what Prince Alexander told you."

Vladimir grimaced. "I implore discretion, Princess."

Payton pushed aside the anger rising inside and moved for the entrance.

Sharp nails sank into her arm as the princess gripped her.

"You have not been excused," she snapped with imperious command.

Payton stared at the woman in disbelief. "You will release my arm at once."

The princess's cheeks were flushed with obvious anger. "Do you know who I am?"

"I have little interest to know. Good day," she said with a nod, yanking her arm away, uncaring that the princess's claws had drawn blood. She had to get away. A sickening sensation had been rioting inside her, and her heart slammed so painfully she felt on the verge of fainting.

"I am Princess Tatiana, Prince Alexander Konstantinovich Dashkova's fiancée."

Payton stumbled, and her stomach hollowed, and unfortunately she did not contain the cry of denial that slipped from her lips.

A light shifted in the depth of the woman's eyes, and if Payton was not mistaken it looked like pity.

She looked away, and her gaze collided with her aunt's.

"It is true; he is a Russian prince, Payton." Her aunt's eyes glowed and she vibrated with excitement. "Better, *your* stable master is the heir to the Dukedom of Avondale."

Her aunt turned to Princess Tatiana. "It is my pleasure to inform you, Prince Mikhail has asked to court my niece, Miss Peppiwell. He would not conduct himself with such dishonor knowing he was committed to another."

While Payton's heart shared such sentiments, it stunned her to witness her aunt's defense of Mikhail.

"Do not be foolish! Prince Alexander would never pursue this unrefined commoner."

The distressing name and title resounded in her head once again. *Prince Alexander. Mikhail is a prince…and a duke?* And he was to marry…a *princess*? It was as if a claw attached itself to her throat and ripped down with brutal precision to her chest. Payton's stomach constricted.

"Excuse me," she said, pushing past the princess, hating the tears gathering behind her eyes.

Outrage twisted in Payton when the princess grabbed her arm again.

"Don't you dare touch me," she snapped low in her throat. "You have been inexcusably rude, and I will not suffer the presence anymore of someone with the manners of a pig. If you thought to confront me because you believe I have some claim on your prince, disabuse yourself of the notion. He is a lying cur like most lords I have been unfortunate to know, and I gladly relinquish him to your venomous embrace."

Liar, her heart screamed, but Payton could not deal with her mind's instinctual rejection of Mikhail being with another woman.

"Impertinent miss!"

Payton inhaled deeply. "Forgive me, that was uncalled for. I had no cause to insult pigs."

Her cheek exploded in fiery pain as the princess slapped her.

The door was flung open, and the duchess entered. "Princess Tatiana," she clipped. "I would invite you to join me in the Rose Room until Prince…" Her voice trailed away when she spied Payton, then regret and apology flashed in Jocelyn's gray eyes. "Payton, I am so sorry," she said softly. "Please do not leave; let me summon Prince Alexander."

Payton flinched. Of course the duchess would have known. She felt like a naive trusting fool. What cause would Mikhail—*Alexander*—have to deceive her so? Tears tightened her throat, but she would be damned if she allowed any to spill. Last night she'd suspected he belonged to the *haute monde*. But she'd thought a baron, or maybe a viscount. But a prince? *Oh God.*

At a loss for what to say, she looked to her aunt and blanched. Aunt Florence's eyes gleamed with avaricious cunning. Mikhail was no longer unworthy. Payton wanted to scream at her aunt's fickleness and her lack of caring for the hurt pummeling Payton. He'd deceived her, misrepresented himself, and they did not care because he was a Russian prince and a duke.

"Please do not, Your Grace," she said formally, and Jocelyn winced. "I am leaving Sherring Cross."

The princess shifted even closer, and Payton wanted to smack the sneer from her face, but suppressed the desire with a will she'd not thought herself capable.

"I believe that is the smart decision, darling. Prince Alexander and I have known each other for years." The princess then rested her hands against her stomach and rubbed in a gentle motion. "There are very compelling reasons he will not be able to marry anyone but me."

Her aunt gasped, and a smug smile appeared on the princess's lips.

"It is very fortunate Vladimir wrote and informed me of Mikhail's fascination with you," Princess Tatiana spat, contempt twisting her features. "Please inform her of what you told me, Vladimir."

He stepped forward, a distinct look of discomfort creasing his handsome face. "Prince Mikhail loves Princess Tatiana, and…and he was merely seeking a distraction with you."

Payton flinched, and the duchess gasped.

Princess Tatiana gave her another sneering smile. "Did you even believe for a second he truly wanted you, a common peasant?"

The room exploded into conversation with the duchess ordering them to be polite or leave her home, her aunt insisting Mikhail would wed her, and the princess hurling insults at Payton.

Payton walked away. Within a few seconds she was outside. She curled her hands into tight fists, desperate to stop their shaking.

Why had he lied? She remembered his words from the picnic: *And what would be your opinion of me, if I confessed to possessing several titles and I am far wealthier than most lords you know?*

She closed her eyes against the memory and the tense way he'd waited for her reply. She had bared her emotions and hurt to him, and he'd still not trusted her. He'd even chosen to inform her father first, no doubt hoping for them to pressure her. The frigid air slapped at her skin, but she was numb to it. Cold rage blossomed in her heart. Once again she had been duped. But this time…this time she had believed. Every uttered lie and sweet false promise of passion and happiness she had welcomed.

How utterly foolish of her.

Mikhail's heart jerked from his chest and lodged in his throat at the tense scene that greeted him in the parlor. He closed his eyes and scrubbed a hand over his face, but Princess Tatiana and her brother were still there when he opened his lids.

He'd strolled from the west wing and made his way to the stables with the intention of riding to the cottage to meet Payton. He'd met her father in London, and Mr. Peppiwell had been very eager to accept Mikhail's proposition to court Payton incognito. Of course the man had only relented after they had drawn up an agreement. Not that Mikhail minded. He was determined to wed Payton. He'd not lingered in London, eager to start his conquest. He'd not been at the ball for long before the vile whispers had started about them. The blast of rage that had filled him had almost made him roar. He'd sought her out and, seeing the torment in her eyes at society's veiled whispers, he'd decided he could not hide his identity and woo her, not when she would suffer until he revealed himself.

The sight of the Arabian horses and Prince Krill's valet in the stables had made Mikhail falter, and the careful speech he had planned explaining his stupidity vanished. He rushed inside to the parlor and shook his head in disbelief when his eyes landed on the immaculately put-together Princess Tatiana Ivanovna.

He allowed his gaze to sweep the room, assessing the rage on the duchess's face, the petulant frown on Princess Tatiana, Vladimir's guilt, and Prince Krill's anger. Yet the only thing that mattered was that Payton was not there when she must have been earlier.

"Where is Payton?" He kept his voice low and calm, lest he betrayed the anger slowly twisting in his gut.

From the tenseness seething in the room, he could imagine what had taken place.

"She fled in tears," Jocelyn said tersely.

Regret sat like a stone in his stomach.

"Why are you here?" he asked, shifting his attention to the princess.

She sent a swift glance toward the duchess.

"Did you offer Payton the courtesy of speaking with her in private...when you flayed her with your words? Why should you be given such favor, when you denied it to her?"

Princess Tatiana turned softened eyes to him. "You judge me without hearing what I have to say?"

"Your satisfied sneer speaks for itself."

She strolled over to him and lifted a hand to touch his face. Revulsion tore through Mikhail, and he jerked from her caress. Impatience bit at him. "Speak as to why you are here."

"Alexander…I love you. I left my pride in Russia and I followed you to England because I need you," she said pleadingly.

They had been friends once, but nothing more. Despite his father's wishes, Mikhail never once gave indication he would welcome something deeper between them. It was laughable she was now speaking words of affection to him. She had always been so sweet, but the lie that she carried his child and insisting they wed was despicable. There had been nothing beneath her sweet softness but emptiness, and greed. After refusing to fall prey to her schemes he'd simply removed her from his thoughts. But to now follow him to England? "How did you know where I was?"

She stepped even closer. "Alexander—"

"How?" His voice snaked through the room like a whip, and she visibly jerked.

Prince Krill shifted, pushing from the wall where he'd been leaning. "Be very careful how you speak to my sister, Alexander," he said, his eyes growing cold in anger.

The duchess glanced to Mikhail and, with a stiff nod to the room in general, she exited.

"After I saw the interest you showed in the American girl, I wrote Princess Tatiana in London, informing her of your whereabouts," Vladimir said stiffly.

Mikhail looked at the man who'd been at his side since his kidnapping and rescue from Madam Anya ten years past. Vladimir had been hired by Mikhail's father, but he thought they'd forged a friendship over the years and that he had the man's loyalty.

"I entrusted you with my confidence, and your response

was to betray me to the princess?"

Vladimir paled. "I did not betray—"

The need to end this unwanted confrontation and be with Payton roiled through him.

"Sherring Cross is not the place for us to have this conversation, Princess. I apologize for leaving home without granting you the audience you sought. If I had acted with courtesy you would not have wasted your time to travel to England. I will be in Wiltshire at my main estate; call on me within the week."

He nodded to Prince Krill and Vladimir. Mikhail moved with purpose, thinking about where Payton would have fled.

"Are you chasing her?" Incredulity rang in the princess's voice.

Mikhail kept walking.

"You will not walk away from me, Alexander, to go to that tramp; I have traveled a long journey to speak with you!"

She rushed to stand in front of the door, her eyes snapping with fear and desperation. "I love you, Alexander. I know I have never told you before, but I have the utmost love and respect for you." She glanced at her brother before lowering her voice. "We can benefit each other. I need a husband, and you do not need a clingy wife who will ask questions. Does your American know of your experience with Madam Anya and the scars with which it left you? Would she be as caring for you if she knew the tales that are alive even today at our court?"

He noted the veiled threat in her tone. "If you approach Payton again I will break you," he said flatly. "And I will show no mercy despite your connection to my family."

Shock flared in her eyes, then doubt. A flicker of calculation entered her gaze before she lowered her lashes.

"Your Payton believes we are engaged and that I am carrying your child. That you were only pursuing her for bed sport. You have your trusted man Vladimir to thank for imparting that wonderful tidbit."

Mikhail stepped close to her, lifting the mask of politeness, and apprehension widened her gaze.

"If you have brought harm to Payton with your thoughtless words I will *never* forgive you."

Princess Tatiana paled. "I am already not in your good graces, so what is one more? And it is you who needs to make amends. I did not lie to her," Princess Tatiana said with a smug smile. "Though I will admit a certain pleasure in shattering whatever naive beliefs she had in relation to you."

With ruthless control, he placed his hands on her hips and lifted her from blocking the door. She squeaked and gripped his arms, her touch knifing him with dread like a poison-tipped dagger. But he did not draw from her, burying all traces of weakness.

"I saw you wrapped in the arms of Prince Dmitri, naked, discussing how to make use of my fortune and the possibility of you passing his child off as mine."

All the blood leached from her face, and she stumbled from Mikhail, gasping. Her brother's face slackened with shock, and he stared at her as if he'd never seen her before.

Mikhail did not care. He wrenched open the door.

"Prince Alexander, I—" Vladimir shook his head, dazed, awareness dawning in his eyes. "Forgive me," he ended stiffly.

Mikhail did not respond, gently closing the door on the silence. He strode down the foyer with quick steps, finally allowing the fear that he'd lost Payton to rear its head.

It was brutal and gripping.

He had no idea what he'd say when he found her. Mikhail only knew he could not let her walk away from the passion and laughter simmering between them because of his blasted stupidity and her misplaced prejudices.

Chapter Fourteen

Payton nearly collapsed with relief when she reached the sanctuary of their cabin. *No.* Just an ordinary cottage. She pulled at the horse's reins, bringing him to a halt, then dismounted. The day was chilly and wet, and a shiver coursed through her. With efficient movements, she tethered Aeton, then fled inside the cottage. A fire blazed in the hearth, casting a golden hue over the cottage, a carafe of wine rested on the small center table, and the room had been aired and cleaned. There was a brown paper lump beside the wine, and she walked over and tore off the wrappings.

She swallowed past the tight lump in her throat. It was an illustrated first edition of *Beauty and the Beast* as told by Jean-Marie Leprince de Beaumont. Payton did not know how long she stood clutching the bound leather book to her chest, her cheeks wet with tears.

The clapping sound of hooves echoed from outside, and a minute later the door to the cottage opened. She could feel his searing gaze, but she did not turn around.

"Leave us and return to the estate," Mikhail said flatly.

She turned to see to whom he spoke and espied Vladimir poised in the doorway of the cottage behind him.

Mikhail moved toward her with purposeful strides.

"Stay where you are," she said hoarsely.

He stopped, regret darkening his eyes. "Payton, I—"

"What is all this?" She lifted the book and pointed to the cleaned room with its fresh curtains and bedsheets.

"I had planned for us to speak here."

Though she knew, she needed to hear it from his lips. "You are titled?"

He schooled his features into a neutral mask, but she could see the guilt in his eyes.

"Yes."

She clenched her hands over the book to prevent their obvious shaking. "You are a prince, a duke, and not a man of affairs or an advisor to Calydon?"

"Payton, I—"

"Answer me!" Her voice came out like a snarl, ferocious enough that he halted the movement of reaching for her.

He flicked a glance to Vladimir, positioned near the entrance of the cottage, pretending he was not listening with rapt interest. With a bow, he gracefully exited and closed the door with a soft snick. The deference shown to Mikhail only served to incense her further.

"You are a prince, and you are engaged to wed a princess." And Payton had almost given him her virtue like a wanton harlot. The clenching pain around her heart was unbearable.

"I am not engaged. Princess Tatiana tried to compromise me into marrying her, and I refused."

She remembered the implication of the princess patting her stomach. "But she is with child."

He stepped closer, and she backed away.

"Her child is not mine, and I have no intention of marrying Princess Tatiana."

Payton was angry at the surge of relief pulsing in her veins. "You told my family of your background, knowing they would pressure me into such an elevated union."

He closed his eyes. "Payton, I—"

"Is your name even Mikhail?"

His jaw visibly clenched. "I am Prince Alexander Mikhail Konstantinovich Dashkova, the Count of Montgomery, and the Duke of Avondale."

Payton's heart pounded. "Why did you lie to me?"

"My reasons for wanting anonymity had nothing to do with you." There was a wealth of pain in his voice that tugged at her heart.

"It was my intention to remain from the prying eyes of society for several months. I simply wanted peace, and I then met you. I...I did not hate the thought of you touching me, and I was not sure what I felt, so I decided to take the time to know you. No woman has ever looked at me and not seen the privileged life I could give her. When we met, Payton, I could see the attraction in your eyes, and you felt this without knowing if I had a farthing to my name. I realized I could pursue you simply as a man and not a prince, a duke, who the *haute monde* was already clamoring to meet, and I acted on the desire. I never meant to hurt you."

And I wanted you because you had no expectation of me to behave in a ladylike fashion. "From what did you want peace?"

"Society," he said flatly. "Scandals, gossips, young ladies doing all in their power to compromise me."

"Thank you for being honest. I will implore you to leave this cottage."

He flinched. "Did you want me when you believed I was an ordinary man?"

Yes. Her throat closed on the answer.

"Tell me you didn't want me then, and I will leave you

alone," he said with shivering intensity.

Payton swallowed, her heart jerking as he started to shrug from his jacket. *Good Heavens.* "Mikhail, I—"

"Answer me," his voice lashed at her.

Emotions clogged her throat. "I wanted you…and I wanted to marry you." She pushed the painful admission past her throat.

"I am the same man, Payton."

How could he believe so? The man standing before her now, although he was dressed casually, had power rolling off him. Penetrating, cool blue eyes stared at her. The change should have been subtle, but the imperious bearing screamed. All the hopes and dreams she had harbored about them in the dark corners of her heart had been smashed into thousands of pieces.

"Maybe," she whispered. "But I have no doubt you would eventually be dissatisfied with your choice."

"An impossibility that is so ludicrous it does not bear discussion. I could never be unhappy with you; you are genuine, a breath of fresh air I want to inhale and keep trapped in my lungs. People always behave differently when they know who I am. All they can see is the title and the wealth. Not me, Payton. They never see *me*. You did."

What about my touch, Mikhail? You said you did not hate my touch, but I still cannot hold you.

He reached for her, and she jerked away. "Your sentiments only drive home your ridiculous reason for deceiving me."

"I…" He thrust his fingers through his hair, and a look of frustration crossed his face. "Do you love me?"

Yes. "What does that matter?"

"I esteem you more than any woman I have ever known."

Not love. Would it have mattered if he spoke of tender feelings? Payton glared at him, unable to credit what she was hearing. "You have insulted me in the worst possible manner, and yet you stand here telling me I should believe that you esteem me?"

His mouth flattened with impatience. "How have I insulted you?"

Temper lit in her veins. "You have touched me, kissed me — " Her voice broke, and she took seconds to rein in her emotions. "You did not trust me with your identity, because you believed me to be the kind of woman to be incapable of holding affection only for you, because you are a prince and a duke. You believed this from our very first meeting. I could understand hiding your titles that first day in the cottage, but you made no effort to confide in me in the days after we met. It is a wonder you want to marry me, when you think so little of my character. You made me believe there was a chance of an *ordinary* life with you. You made me yearn for your kisses, hunger for your touch, dream of having a son with your eyes, a daughter with your smile, knowing you would never be able to give me the life I desire…a life you were fully aware I craved. This only reveals to me you care so little for the things I desire for my life."

He flinched, and an emotion akin to despair flashed in the depth of his eyes. "Give me a chance to make amends. It was never my intention to hurt you, and I swear I will do all in my power to give you the life you crave. I have enough wealth so you can live how you please, do whatever you desire."

Was such a thing possible with him? Her heart wavered, and she snapped her spine straight. A few pretty words would not make her resolve change. "No."

A ruthless determination settled on his face. "Is there the possibility you can love me?"

I fear I already do. She shook her head in confusion. "What do you want from me?"

"Marry me, be my princess, my duchess, and I swear you will never want for anything."

Pain twisted in her heart. He was a prince, a duke; he would rub shoulders with the highest of the *haute monde*. She would *never* fit into his world. She wanted to scream at him. Everything had been so perfect when he had been common. "I am not polished enough to be your princess or your duchess. You will be called to court and Parliament, be expected to host balls and political meetings, and I cannot envision such a life for myself."

His eyes were steady on Payton; her carefully constructed mask of indifference was on the verge of crumbling.

"Then simply be my wife…my lover, and my friend."

An inarticulate murmur slipped from her at the raw hunger in his eyes. *Yes*, her heart screamed, but her lips would not agree. The anxiety of trapping herself in such a world clamped around her heart, but the dread of losing him forever made her knees wobble. "I need time to think," she gasped hoarsely.

He prowled closer; the sheer force of his magnetism and will pressed in on her, arousing fear and the heady sense of primal desire in equal measure.

He cupped her cheeks, the gentleness of his touch at odds with the emotions that darkened his gaze to cobalt. He pressed a kiss to her forehead, and her breath hitched. Tilting her head more, he kissed her, a simple meeting of lips, an exchange of breath, without demand. "Be my lover and wife, Payton. That is all I ask. I will shield you from everything else." His voice was a low soothing murmur, coaxing her to say yes and succumb to all the temptations and delight he had to offer.

She reached up and clasped the hands cupping her cheeks, and he froze. Denial roiled through her blood. "Except my touch. You said you also pursued me because you did not hate the idea of me touching you. But you still deny me the pleasure of learning you, threading our fingers together as we stroll by the lake, the comfort of holding you when you despair, the simple joy of hugging you when I am happy." She dropped her hand, a different type of pain pulling at her heart. "Tell me, Mikhail, will you allow me to touch you eventually?"

Awful silence.

She tried to step back, and he drew her close.

"No, do not pull from me," he said, kissing the corner of her mouth.

Awareness hummed in her veins. "I must. You tempt me with a life in which I know I will find despair."

"I am falling in love with you, Payton. You are the first woman to make me hunger for the feel of your touch, the first to make me laugh so easily, and the only one to make me dream of idle days by the fire, or in bed, wrapped around you, drowning in your scent as I drive you to completion. You tempt me to relinquish control to you. Never before have I possessed such thoughts."

A dangerous thrill shot through her and, before she could respond, he kissed her. She allowed the fire of lust to consume her world, willingly burning away the doubt and hurt, to only bask in the moment of sheer pleasure, for she would never again feel such joy in a man's arms.

His lips devoured her, and he stroked his tongue in her mouth with ruthless persuasion. But his touch at her nape and hip was a gentle caress, a soothing glide over her fevered flesh in the midst of the storm into which his sensual assault drew her.

She clasped his shoulders, and he pulled from her. Gripping her hands, he kissed her knuckles, then lowered them to her side and pushed them behind her, holding her hands at her back in a gentle but ironclad clasp. The move thrust her breast outward, an offering for him to touch and taste.

"I cannot allow you to touch me." Regret and pain swirled

in his gaze.

Her heart thudded. "I know," she said.

"I am going to take you."

A soft whimper escaped her lips. "I know."

"And I will bind you to my bed when I do so."

Danger and anticipation prickled along her senses. "Once again you are speaking too much."

His low laugh created a sweet ache that filled her chest. He released her hands and stepped away from her. Then he tugged at his simple cravat, pulling it from his neck. His eyes, glittering and aroused, pinned her to the spot. Mikhail moved behind her, unbuttoned and unlaced her corset and the tapes to her petticoats, and pushed them from her hips. In complete silence he removed stays, chemise, stockings, and drawers. Payton trembled when she stood wantonly naked, his comforting weight pressing into her from behind.

"Everything in me is urging me to lift you to the bed and place you on your knees and elbows, sink my cock into you, and give you pleasure until you are trembling from the intensity," he said softly at her nape, licking along the arch of her throat.

The images that erupted in Payton's mind had a distinct appeal, and her breathing fractured, and in utter shock she could feel the moisture pooling between her legs.

"But I find I cannot bear the idea of not seeing your eyes, your face blushing with passion, another anomaly I endure when it comes to you, Payton."

He encircled her wrists, and the silken press of his cravat glided against her skin as he bound her wrists together at her back. Her awareness of him was acute and intense.

He tugged, testing the knot's firmness. Then he removed the pins from her hair, tumbling the heavy coil to her lower back. He glided around her and barely placed his lips against hers. The caress was subtle, but Payton felt as if he breathed her in.

"If you ever want me to release your bonds, call me Alexander."

Then the kiss grew deeper, and her heart raced, for the intensity of his mouth as it roved over hers bespoke need, a claiming.

He glided the tips of his fingers over her hips, up her side with firm pressure, leaving fire in his wake. She moaned, leaning farther into his caress, instinctively tugging at the restraints, needing to twine herself around him and hold him to her.

She sobbed into his kiss as the visceral need was denied, but was drawn into a vortex of pulse-pounding pleasure as he ravaged her lips.

He cupped her breast, flicking a thumb over her straining nub. Oh, his touch. *It is glorious.* Her nipple beaded, and the delicious throb started low between her thighs. As if he sensed her rising need, he nudged her legs wide, snaked his hand down, and cupped her most intimate part. Then he stroked her, and Payton's knees nearly gave.

She pulled from their kiss, dropping her forehead to his shoulder as he continued his wicked torment. His fingers were magical as he strummed and caressed her straining knot of pleasure, before sliding two fingers deep…and deliciously hard.

He murmured soothing reassurances when she jerked at the sharp lash of pleasure and pain. Payton arched, lifting to her toes, and bit into his shoulder through his jacket, a sob of need hissing through her teeth.

"Release my hands," she pleaded with a whimper. She desperately needed an anchor, needed to touch him, to hold onto anything that would help her ride the waves of sensations coursing through her body.

"No."

Mikhail nudged her legs wide and pushed his fingers deeper, stroking her over and over. The sensations peaked in her belly, and she started to tremble. On a wordless cry, Payton let ecstasy consume her, shuddering as waves of release rolled through her.

"Are you well?" The sensual rasp of his voice calmed her, soothing the edges of raw need that still lingered.

"You are still clothed." Her voice was thick with arousal.

He eased from her, and she glanced up into his shuttered eyes.

What is it?

He removed his waistcoat and shirt with quick movements, baring his wonderfully sculpted chest. She gasped as he gripped her by the hips and lifted. Payton instinctively circled his thighs with her legs to prevent herself from falling. Her bound hands did not allow her to clasp him for purchase. Strong arms came around her back and hips, holding her to him until he settled into the winged-back chair near the fire.

He eased her off his lap ever so slightly and undid the buttons to his trousers. It was then she realized he would not fully undress, that he would eschew all form of skin on skin contact, for he settled her on his thighs and positioned her so she could not lean on his naked flesh.

A hard brush of velvet steel caressed against her, and she lowered her eyes to his lap.

Her breath caught audibly at his thick length. She wanted to explore him, to feel his vitality in her palm. The ache in her heart grew unbearable.

"I wish…"

He skimmed a light caress over her trembling lips. "I know," he said, his voice low and rough, but unyielding.

He lowered his hand from her cheek, leaned forward and reached behind her, gripping the middle of the tied cravat. Then he pulled her into him and slanted his lips over hers.

They kissed tenderly...and deeply. With a soft moan she parted her lips for him, allowing the passion to sweep her away, burying the flare of hurt of not being able to touch him.

His other hand slid over her buttocks and squeezed, before drifting around to her heated center, sliding a finger deep, never releasing her lips from their heated embrace.

It was the only part of her he allowed to cling to him with such fervor, and even as she trembled at the devastating pleasure peaking with every slide and dip of his fingers, she coaxed his lips to never release hers. Each kiss went deeper, lingered longer, connecting them on a more profound level of intimacy than she'd ever explored with him. Each kiss communicated regret and longing, hurt and acceptance. And God help her, but she felt the burning love.

The steady drops of rain against the windows, his taste, his scent, the beat of her heart, the firm caress against her nub of pleasure pounded delight through her veins. Her eyes fluttered open and she rode the pleasure, staring into the dark desire in his eyes.

He shifted, widening her legs bracketing his thighs, and the thick, broad edge of his erection nudged at her soft wetness. A dull aching pulse began to throb between her thighs. Sweat coated her skin; she trembled on him and, with a soft sigh, she arched and let him in, accepting the penetration.

For she could do nothing but submit to the yearning desire simmering between them.

Chapter Fifteen

Mikhail needed to obliterate the pain in her golden eyes, wanted to brand her with passion so she was not capable of leaving. The relentless need to claim her irrevocably as *his*, rose hot and powerful inside. She was becoming everything to him, and he did not want to lose her, not her stubbornness, her fierce pride, or her captivating mix of vulnerability and strength.

Her hair, as rich as autumn leaves, flowed down her back, and her eyes glowed with wanton heat. Holding her gaze, he pulled her onto his aching length slowly and relentlessly. She was so damned tight. Sweat beaded his brow. Her teeth sank into her plump bottom lip, and her beautiful eyes glittered with apprehension and arousal. Mikhail slid his hand along the curves of her thighs, worshipping the feel of her lush body, up to her hips, round to the globes of her ass where he tightened his grip.

A sob hitched in her throat, but he did not stop. He had ensured he brought her to pleasure so she was wet enough to take his thick length.

"Arch your breast to me."

Her eyes widened but she complied. The move pressed her sweat-drenched body against his chest. He groaned at the friction of her bare skin rasping against his, a primitive triumph twisting inside, for the sensation did not repel him. Her nipples were a dusky pink, and he took a hardened nipple between his teeth and bit, before rolling it gently and sucking. She damn well purred, then shivered on his cock, bathing him in liquid heat.

A strangled groan escaped Mikhail's lips. The feel of her slick heated flesh slowly engulfing the crest of his cock nearly drove him to his knees. Pleasure rippled from his engorged length to his balls.

"Marry me, Payton."

Her eyes flared. "No."

He'd never felt this lust curling through him with another woman. He clenched his teeth against the searing pleasure. The edges of his control frayed, he coasted his hands up to the curve of her back, hugging her close to him, and drew her down to meet his upward plunge.

"Mikhail!"

Her cry echoed in the cottage. She tugged at her wrists, but the knotted cravat held firm. He brushed his thumb over her trembling lips. Then without any urging from him, she rode him slowly, rolling her hips in a rhythm that was instinctively sensual and decadent.

Mikhail gripped her hips, encouraging her wicked motions, and she groaned. Need coiled hot and intense through him. He wanted everything.

"Mikhail." Her moans poured through the air as she rocked on his length.

Lust rippled through him at the picture she presented, her hands bound, her back arched, the graceful curve of her throat on tantalizing display, her tangled hair rippling down her back and cascading over his knees, her skin sweat-drenched. She was so beautiful.

He lifted her and dropped her down on his length with strength. A low, keening cry broke from her throat as he seated her fully on his cock. He stood with her, tugging at the knots at her wrists to loosen them. He tumbled with her to the bed, keeping his weight on his arms. "Grip the pillows and do not release them."

She gasped, growing even wetter, and he groaned low in his throat. She was so wonderfully responsive.

"Wrap your legs around my hips."

Her eyes flared, and a sensual smile curved her lips. She complied, and he withdrew and plunged into her with the full force of his desire driving him. She whimpered but her flesh parted to take him, and she arched her hips into his ravenous thrusts. He pressed his nose into the hollow at the base of her neck and let his world catch fire.

Mikhail drowned himself in the maddening bliss of being surrounded by her wet heat. He made love to her fiercely, taking and giving, driving into her with a pounding rhythm that shook the cot against the wall. There was a distant clang in his head to remember her innocence, but she did not allow it with her whispered moans and pleas for more. Her breathing grew ragged, and she undulated underneath him with raw carnality, gripping his cock in the tightest, wettest clasp he'd ever experienced.

She was a sensualist, and she was *his*.

When the bliss claimed her, she clamped her supple legs around his waist, restricting his motions, burning him with cold ice at the feel of being trapped. She yelled her pleasure, and he lifted from the crook of her neck and claimed her lips. He rode her through her orgasm, and she sobbed and moaned all of her delight and need into his kiss, drawing his passion from him. He bit into the soft of her lips as he tumbled with her.

Payton's heart raced, and sweat slicked her skin. She fought the sense of drowsy contentment and glanced at Mikhail. It was very difficult for her to remain distant and to hold onto the betrayal that had shafted her insides when they were entwined so intimately.

He lay on top of her, cradled between her thighs, holding his weight off her by resting on one of his elbows. His other hand cupped her cheek, and she could not tear herself from the intensity of his stare.

"I can see the distance in your eyes," he said softly.

"And I can feel it in your touch."

His muscles locked, and her heart pounded.

"This was farewell, Mikhail." She pushed the words past the lump in her throat.

He held her gaze for the longest time, not speaking or protesting. His blue eyes darkened with an emotion she was unable to decipher. Lacing his fingers through hers, he pressed her hands above her head and shifted between her thighs.

She gasped as she felt the broad length of him against her tender entrance. Without releasing her from the power of his mesmerizing gaze, he thrust deep and embedded himself in one hard stroke. The cry strangled in her throat. She felt deliciously impaled, the penetration stretching her despite the wetness of her flesh. But the shocking and devastating thing was the brutal punch of pleasure that roared inside her and shattered her into pieces.

A low, sensual chuckle came from him.

Heat dusted her cheeks. He had brought her to pleasure from simply entering her body. She tugged at her hands, and he released them. She wound her hands around his neck, tugging his lips to hers. "This does not mean anything," she whispered hoarsely.

He froze, and it was a dagger to her heart. She slowly slipped her hands from his skin and fisted them in the sheets.

"Wrong," he murmured, then withdrew and plunged deep, sinking her hips into the mattress, without breaking the connection of their stare. "The way you bathe my cock with your pleasure, the ecstasy you feel at my touch, the pleasure that wrapped around my heart from simply breathing in your scent, is *everything*." His voice was dark as sin. Then he withdrew and snapped his hips forward with shocking strength.

A sob clawed from Payton's throat at the devastating pleasure.

"This means everything," he said, then he took her lips in a kiss so soft and gentle she quaked.

Though his lips and tongue coaxed and soothed her, the rhythm of his hips as he loved her was untamed. She wanted to coast her hands over his shoulders, feel the ripple of his muscles under her palm, bite the cord of his neck, and taste the sweat on his skin.

"Please let me touch you," she breathed. "I will go slowly."

"No." His refusal was a pained moan and a piercing to her heart. She could not imagine a life where she never held him.

"I want to run my arms over your shoulders, your back, your buttocks, I want to feel the sweat on your skin, the power in your body as you push your c-cock into me over and over," she tempted against his lips on a soft purr.

"No."

His lips denied her, but his eyes were a dam of need so powerful, she expected it to crash over her at any moment and drown her.

"Let me taste you," she said, and bent her head to nip his shoulders.

"No."

"I cannot bear not holding you."

"If you want me to stop, you've only to say the word."

Alexander. Yet it was "Mikhail," she gasped, as his thrusts grew rougher, more demanding, and she slid deeper into bliss, burying her face against his neck, and sliding her hands against the silken sheets to once more grip the pillow, desperate for a firmer anchor.

His hips snapped harder and deeper, and every nerve ending in Payton came alive with pleasure and erotic pain. He captured her lips in a fierce kiss and thrust, once, twice, and on the third plunge her entire body shuddered under the onslaught of bliss.

"Look at me." His voice was a growl.

She lifted her eyes to his.

Please, she silently begged, *let me touch you.*

She couldn't break the power of his stare, the demand to be connected on such a level as they tumbled into ecstasy.

A rumble of thunder echoed in the cottage, and the cool air chilled the sweat on her skin. She trembled, and he shifted, drawing the blanket over them, cocooning her in blissful warm, yet false, intimacy. He pulled her to him, so close she could feel the heat, yet he was careful they did not touch. She remained silent, floating in a haze of pleasure, trying to ignore the questions prodding her mind, and the raw pain in her heart. The fire turned to ash yet they did not move or speak.

"How long has it been since you welcomed another's touch?"

His breathing did not change, nor did he stiffen, but she swore she could feel the tension weaving itself through his muscles.

"Ten years."

Her stomach knotted. She wanted to soothe the emptiness she heard in his voice. She slid her hand across the silken sheets without looking in his direction. She held her breath when the side of her hand bumped into his. Payton slowly relaxed when he did not flinch or shift away. A small smile lifted her lips, for this was the first time she had touched him, though it was the lightest of touches, and he'd not flinched. "I am deeply sorry, Mikhail."

Silence.

"Will you tell me?"

He tensed. "When I was sixteen I was kidnapped."

Her breath hitched.

"My father was a friend and great supporter of the Emperor of Russia, Alexander II. Our emperor was hated for some of his bold political successes, and there were those who sought to undermine him. It was hard for their arms to reach and influence the emperor himself, so they turned to those close to him, their families, seeking a weakness to exploit. Once they found that weakness, they would have then used Alexander's supporters to infiltrate where they could not. A group of people who years later formed the Narodnaya Volya, turned their eyes on my father's family and activities."

Mikhail glided his fingers over her hand beside his, and then finally locked them together.

"I was taken, and while the ransom for information was sent to my father, I was held in a brothel, a place they were sure the authorities would never look to find me. I was tied to a bed, hand and foot, waiting to be rescued. Hours later, the Madam of the house—Anya—came into the room. It seems she just had not been able to resist me, or resist bringing in her clients, men and women to use me. No threat I used could discourage her, and despite the disgust, shame, and rage I felt, nothing prevented me from responding to their vile touches. I was with her…and them…for several days before my father's man arrived."

The echoes of rage and pain in his tone had Payton biting her lower lip. She gripped their clasped hands and lifted them to her lips where she pressed a kiss to his knuckles. "You do not have to tell me anymore," she said hoarsely.

"I can hear the tears in your voice, Payton. I forbid you to pity me."

Tears rolled down her cheeks, her mind alive with imagining such violations. "I do not pity you. I am deeply sorry—"

His hand tightened on hers.

"Nor will you express sentiments of regret, for you had no hand in causing my pain."

She nodded, lifting their laced hands to once again kiss his knuckles.

"Are they dead?"

He chuckled. "Bloodthirsty little thing, aren't you?" Then a beat later he said, "They were punished to the full extent of the law."

"I am glad," she said softly.

Was this why he had suffered society's displeasure? She had a multitude of questions roiling through her, but she tempered them. It could not have been easy for him to confide such a painful experience. It would not do for her to badger him with questions when she could feel the dreadful tension seething from him.

"My kidnapping and torture was a vile scandal that lived in my court for years. I could not bear the touch of another, and it became evident, as I would withdraw from every embrace, or brush of skin, deliberate or accidental. I could not survive allowing anyone close unless *I* allowed it. I was betrothed to Lady Olga, yet upon my return I could not endure her closeness. Months passed and I still could not. I found her in the arms of another. I understood, and I did not hate her for it, but it made me realize I may never be able to experience normal intimacy."

Oh.

"Scandal has been a part of my life for as long as I can remember. Princess Tatiana compounded it by painting me as a seducer of the worst sort. When I arrived in England, I knew how it would be, the *haute monde* watching and waiting, young ladies behaving silly just to garner my attention or entrap me. I wanted a break from it all, so I had thoughts to bury myself in Sherring Cross. Then I met you…"

Scandal.

She tightened her fingers on his, and with a tug he pulled from her.

Though she understood, it still hurt.

"I do not know if I will ever be able to suffer your touch," he admitted in a bleak tone.

Suffer…

She nodded, her throat tight with emotion. How could she ever hope to overcome such memories?

He drew her to him, and though she was sore, she did not protest when he flipped her to her stomach and covered her like a warm sensual blanket, nudging her legs apart with his to slide his thick length impossibly deep within her once again. The groan that pulled from her throat was echoed by Mikhail.

His breath tickled her ear. "Do you believe you will ever consent to walk in my world?"

She closed her eyes and gasped as a tear leaked from her lids. "No." Their fierce loving had not changed anything. He was still a prince, a duke…and she was still woefully ordinary.

She shifted and grasped the fingers he had clenched on the pillow above her head. His muscles tensed above, and he trembled. It was subtle, but she felt it.

Her heart broke just a bit more. "You cannot bear my touch, Mikhail, and I cannot survive the pain, scandal, and hypocrisy of your world. Why should we trap each other in such an impossible situation?"

Please show me the way, she silently begged.

He remained silent, and she felt when he retreated emotionally from her.

Farewell, Mikhail.

Chapter Sixteen

Cold rain fell in a steady drizzle, wetting him, but Mikhail did not care. He stood on the small front porch of the cottage, gazing into another starless night, Vladimir at his side. Mikhail had woken the second Payton roused from her exhausted slumber. He'd watched her observing him through slitted eyes, pain and regret darkening her lovely features.

The heaviness in his heart was an unbearable weight. *You cannot bear my touch…why should we trap each other in such an impossible situation?*

She'd dressed as best she could without assistance and then fled the cottage, racing away on Aeton. He'd dressed, appreciating the coldness encasing his heart. It pushed against the dart of slashing pain stuck within. Mikhail could not guess how long he'd remained outside in the cold before Vladimir had ridden to join him.

"Miss Peppiwell has left Sherring Cross," Vladimir said into the quiet of the night.

"I know."

"Forgive me for interfering in a situation I had not

comprehended," Vladimir said hoarsely. "The princess is a friend, and I believed her, when I should have known you would never act with such dishonor."

Mikhail remained silent.

"Won't you go after Miss Peppiwell?"

"I told her of Madam Anya, but Payton still left."

The man's eyes widened, and the awareness of what Payton meant to him must have penetrated, for Vladimir blanched.

"Forgive my interference."

"The fault does not lie with you…but with me. Society bows to my wealth and influence, but she does not care for it."

I will not survive your world. She had sounded so final, yet she had given herself to him. Even now she could be with his child. Fierce possessiveness gripped Mikhail's heart.

"That is very unusual," Vladimir said.

Yes, one of the very aspects that had drawn him to her fire was also serving to keep her from him.

Another rider emerged from the dark, and Calydon brought his horse to a stop and dismounted.

"Leave us," Mikhail ordered.

With a nod, Vladimir departed, greeting Calydon before mounting his horse and riding back to the house.

His cousin approached with measured steps, his eyes assessing Mikhail.

"Payton has left Sherring Cross. Her parents are firmly on her heels, no doubt eager to drag her back to accept your offer."

Mikhail grunted.

"I am certain you have more to say," Calydon said with a lifted brow.

He joined him on the steps, a bottle of brandy clutched firmly in his hands. Calydon handed it to him, and Mikhail took a deep swig, letting the burn slide down his throat and settle in his belly.

"Will you go after her?"

"No." He had seen the pain in her eyes when he did not allow her to touch him. It had been the same with Lady Olga, and she had only withstood the distance for a few months before breaking from him in tears. How long would it take Payton?

"Why not?"

"She does not want me." *Impossible*, his heart taunted. The woman who had surrendered to him so sweetly, with such ardor, needed him, just not the trappings of society.

"Is it because of what happened with Madam Anya?"

"Yes...no... Who the hell knows?" *You are a prince and that is the only reason she is rejecting you.* And the most painful part of his admission was that he understood. There had been days when he walked through the halls of the Russian court, and the rabid and shocked whispers had gutted him. When his aversion to touch had been realized by those he flinched from—his family and friends—pity had been mixed with the curiosity, urging him to shun society. But he'd refused to bow to weakness and had shrouded himself in cold distance from it all—pity, curiosity, love, and understanding. "Payton believes there is no hope for us. She cannot imagine being my princess and duchess, and she does not believe I will ever be able to endure her touch."

He handed the bottle of brandy to Calydon.

"You can force society to accept her."

"I do not want to," Mikhail said. "I would prefer to show Payton she does not need society's approval, and it is hers they will need to gain. As my princess, my duchess, she will have more influence that she can comprehend."

His cousin smiled fleetingly. "And what of her other concern?"

Mikhail's gut clenched. "I have a great urge to submit

myself to Payton's caresses," he admitted. "But I cannot imagine giving someone such power over my desire again."

Calydon threw him a surprised look, and Mikhail understood. The control he had learned to exercise over his passion had been absolute.

"In what way?" the duke asked with curiosity rife in his tone.

Mikhail hesitated. Though he trusted and respected Calydon it was hard for him to bare his emotions.

"With Payton I do not have the hard-won control I worked so hard to attain." He gritted his teeth, almost uncomfortable in telling his cousin what he had done. But Calydon needed to understand how disturbed Mikhail felt, and how significant Payton's effect was on him.

"When I turned twenty-one, I revisited Madam Anya."

"The hell you say!"

The cold memories of the time before, when he had been sixteen and at the madam's brutal mercy slithered through Mikhail, leaving a vile taste in his mouth.

"I did return. After my Cossack riders tore the brothel apart and found me…" He scrubbed a hand over his face and across his nape with unnecessary roughness. It was as if he wanted to remove the lingering memory of her touch, the licks of her tongue, and the whip as it bit into his skin, leaving behind the sickening sensations of pain with pleasure.

He grabbed back the bottle and took another swig. "I spent years training, honing my body into a weapon. Never did I want to be at the mercy of another being again. And if I found myself in such a position, it would be with the full awareness I had done everything physically, and mentally I was capable of outwitting them."

He went silent, thinking of how he had cut himself off from physical pleasures unless he commanded it. He had never allowed anyone close, friends or family. "I built such control over my physical reactions that I would only become aroused if I allowed it. And I allowed it a lot," he admitted with a wry chuckle. "I took dozens of lovers, the raw need in me demanding to wipe away the memory of Anya's touch, but on my terms."

"Why the hell did you place yourself at her mercy again?" Calydon demanded, anger riding his voice. "Did she hurt you?" he growled.

Mikhail glanced at him. "I wanted to prove I had the utmost control over my passion. I had her released from prison and taken back to the brothel with orders to make herself presentable. She knew someone from the *Dvoryanstvo* was visiting, so she pampered and prepared her body, no doubt hoping to secure a powerful protector who could rescue her from the hell in which she had been wallowing. When I stepped through the door…I never beheld a woman more beautiful. Of course she did not understand. I laid it out for her in clear terms. Please me, arouse my body, and then ride me to fulfillment, and she would be freed from the life imprisonment sentence that had been handed to her."

"Christ," Sebastian snarled.

"I sat on the chaise in her boudoir and suffered her ministration. An hour later, despite all her licking, teasing, and sucking, my cock remained flaccid. In her desperation she suggested I was impotent. That my time with her before had broken me."

Memories twisted, and he frowned, surprised the disgust he normally felt had been reduced somewhat.

"Why the hell have you stopped?" Sebastian snapped. "Finish your story."

Mikhail chuckled mirthlessly. "A second later, my cock stood to attention because *I* commanded my body to feel. To be aroused by her sensuality."

His cousin was silent, staring at him. Then he asked, "Lady

Olga?"

You are cold... Did you not think your actions would drive me to find comfort elsewhere? Lady Olga had cried, tears streaming down her cheeks, her eyes wide pools of fear and hurt, when he'd learned of her sleeping with a count. Mikhail had then tried to allow her to touch him. Nausea had churned in his gut, and cold sweat had drenched his skin within seconds. "I did not allow her touch, either, nor allow her kisses unless I granted it. And during the length of our engagement, my want for her or any other woman was nonexistent. I was content with the emptiness, and I never knew I hungered for normalcy until it was at my fingertips."

Calydon sighed. "Payton."

Just hearing her name stirred visceral need inside of Mikhail. She aroused his mind, body, and soul, but he knew he would not be able to bear her touch because of his damnable weakness. He should let her go. "Yes...Payton."

"And her touch disgusts you as well?"

No. The burn of dread had been different. More unusual and strange than terrible. There had been no nausea, no shaking, and no nightmares. *And I was a blasted fool to let her leave.* How could he have thought to relinquish her smiles, her vivacity, and the beauty of everything about her? "I crave her caresses even when I despair the ill feeling that will come with someone touching me without permission."

He faced his cousin. "I do not think I can relinquish her. Even if it means I will not be able to suffer her touch for years to come. The possibility of a life with her is worth the risk." Mikhail's heart pounded unmercifully. Would a woman like Payton accept she could never touch him, possibly for months, years? Would Payton eventually turn to another man for her needs?

Never.

She would prefer to suffer in cold silence with him. And

Mikhail admitted he might never possess the willpower to let her go. "Am I a selfish bastard for wanting to trap her in a life she hates?"

"No."

"I am willing to live in a simple cottage and eschew all of society for her happiness. I confess even such an idea is appealing."

Calydon nodded in apparent approval. "The generous woman I know Payton to be, she will love you unreservedly. Fight for her, show her how life with you can be. I know your ruthlessness, Mikhail. Employ it so she never suffers the brunt of society's displeasure."

He knew what he needed to do...submit to her touch, and discover if there was hope.

The carriage rocked and swayed, carrying Payton away from Sherring Cross, away from the temptation of Mikhail. She locked her heart against the need to return to him. She'd informed no one of her departure, only packing a small valise. Jocelyn had seen her determination and offered a carriage. Payton wiped at the tears streaming down her face in annoyance. She had decided to leave, so why was she hurting so much?

Marry me.

God, she wanted to, despite knowing she would never fit into his world, despite knowing the lifelong scrutiny she would be placed under, despite not really knowing the man behind the title. Surely she would come to regret it. Surely she would eventually be an embarrassment with her lack of social graces.

Breathing deeply, she struggled to quiet her mind, allowing the exhaustion to carry her under. She had been traveling for at least an hour now and should arrive in London shortly. Though she feared that was not enough time to forget Mikhail, his kisses, his touch, the devastating pleasure he had introduced her to.

Trying to direct her thoughts to less painful musings, she tugged her sketchpad out and started to draw a similar cottage to their own. She could see setting a story there, one where children enter and were transported into a magical world. Time passed as she immersed herself in the drawings of the cottage, a portal, and the five intrepid children seeking adventure. Tonight she would fill in the words to complement the illustrations.

The closer she drew to London and to Connie and Lucan's town house on upper Brook Street, the more Payton's disquiet grew. Connie had recently married the Duke of Mondvale amidst much scandal. Since then, she had been a reigning toast for taming the man known to all as the *Lord of Sin*, and many clamored to be invited to the exclusive dinner parties and soirees she hosted. She had badgered Payton relentlessly to attend one of her rare balls; Payton had kept declining.

She had grudgingly left a note to her mother and aunt, informing them where she traveled. Payton would hate for them to launch an investigation and a manhunt into her disappearance, otherwise she doubted she would have informed her family of her departure. She loved them, but they also frustrated and hurt her deeply with their lack of support. They would be rabid because of her refusal to marry Mikhail, and her father would be certain to disinherit her for refusing a prince and a duke.

Am I being foolish?

She'd forgiven Mikhail's deception, for she understood what it was like to be judged and measured not as the person one really was. He was a wealthy, titled aristocrat used to people toadying to his comforts, never being challenged or admired just for who he really was. While he was revered for his wealth and his ancestral heritage, she was derided for lacking what society called breeding. She had felt that no one ever took the time to peer beneath the veil into her heart. She knew it must be the same emotions and needs that had driven him to want to appear to be ordinary with her.

It was startling to feel the bittersweet ache of kinship with Mikhail.

Did she truly love him? The very idea seemed improbable. Lord Jensen had wooed and courted her for eight months before she had admitted to feeling some affection for him. She had only been with Mikhail a total of seven days, and she wanted to lay her heart and soul down before him. The idea terrified her.

Too emotionally exhausted to think further, she closed her eyes, allowing the rocking of the carriage to take her away from her troubled thoughts into deep slumber.

Chapter Seventeen

Payton doubted she had ever attended such a crush. The Duchess of Mondvale's ball was a smashing success. Payton had arrived on Connie's doorstep and had promptly burst into tears when her magnetic and too dashing husband, Lucan Wynwood, had opened the front door.

The tears had mortified Payton. She was not the type of female to give in to bouts of crying and vapors, but the man had been unruffled and had drawn her inside and hugged her. She had flung her arms around him, strangely glad to be able to return a comforting embrace.

His beautiful and vibrant duchess had bundled her into a guest chamber where they had spent the night talking. Payton had slid into an exhausted slumber, passing the day and majority of the following afternoon cocooned in sleep.

She roused late in the afternoon to realize she had arrived on the eve of the ball. Connie refused to accept the explanation that Payton was without a gown. They were of a similar build, so Payton had reluctantly agreed to accept one of the most glorious dresses she had ever worn.

The gown was of deep rose silk with an overskirt of silver gauze. A thick band of the rose silk encircled her tiny waist and the off-the-shoulder bodice was made in the same silk covered with silver gauze. The neckline, scalloped hem of the overskirt, and tiny sleeves were embroidered with flowers in delicate seed pearls. Her dark hair was arranged high around a cluster of roses of the palest pink in shades darkening to the pink of her dress. Her dancing slippers matched the dress, and her fan was of silver lace, embroidered with golden threads.

She had not even been at the ball for half an hour when the first whisper reached her ear.

Jilted.

Horse breeder.

Instead of hurting, her lips twitched. Society was too predictable, and it just might be possible she was becoming immune to their vicious tongues. But the greater amusement was wondering how they would react when they discovered her horse breeder was Prince Alexander Dashkova, the Duke of Avondale.

She collected a glass of champagne from a passing footman, hoping for a cool breeze to soothe the heat of the crush. The terrace doors were open, and there had been a definite nip in the air earlier in the day. All that had been stifled under the multitude of guests mingling and laughing in the duke's grand ballroom.

Payton stood on the sidelines, content no one had asked her to dance. Connie was playing the charming yet reserved hostess, and everyone was lapping it up, pleased to garner her attention if only for a few seconds.

How fickle society was. Months ago all Connie had been to them was the beautiful bastard, and no one had wanted to be her friend.

With a snort Payton lifted the glass to her lips and drank.

"…she is Mr. Marcus Stone's mistress, and the duchess still

calls her friend," a voice rife with appalled shock said, and with a sigh, Payton glanced toward the unfortunate female. A smile burst on her lips, as she identified Lady Charlotte Ralston, Connie's dearest friend.

"*Are you certain? She converses with my daughter, Lady Ophelia, frequently. I must stop such corrupting influence at once.*"

"*There is a rumor she has been seen leaving the man's apartment at his gambling club, Decadence, and her lady's maid told my lady's maid Lady Ralston may be with child!*"

Payton's chest ached. She already knew how this gossip would take little or no time to spread and would create a circle of pain and heartache. She pushed through the crowd, toward Charlotte.

"Prince Alexander Konstantinovich Dashkova, His Grace, the Duke of Avondale, and the Countess of Merryweather," the butler's voice boomed, announcing Mikhail and—mystifyingly—her aunt.

Oh God.

Payton faltered and lifted her eyes to the grand staircase with the rest of the guests. He was every bit the arrogant and powerful aristocrat, once again dressed in sharp elegant black-and-white evening wear. It was only as he came closer that she realized his waistcoat was silver, almost as if he had known what color her dress would be.

Connie went over and greeted him, and the crowded assembly surged, no doubt eager to arrange introductions and form the connection. Unerringly his gaze found hers, and her breath caught at the possessive way his eyes lingered.

She swallowed as he pulled away from everyone and prowled toward her. Even Connie looked baffled until she saw the direction he headed, then an enchanting smile split her face, and she gave Payton an audacious wink.

Good heavens.

Mikhail was making no effort to disguise the passion he felt for her.

It was shockingly outrageous…and wonderful.

Her heart raced in earnest. It was then she realized how quiet everyone was, and the prickling sensation of being watched by so many eyes rippled over her skin with discomfort, one that melted away the second he stopped in front of her.

"Miss Peppiwell," he greeted, and bowed over her hand, then he lifted darkening blue eyes to her face.

Memories of his tongue against her, his hands pleasuring, and his overwhelming magnetism had a soft breath shuddering from her. Her heart ached. *If only.*

"My dear," her aunt said, from behind him. "Please greet your intended."

How could she? Did Aunt Florence really believe the court of society's opinion meant so much to Payton? There were several shocked gasps and rage burned through her. How dare they? She had said no, and her family knew very well she had meant every word.

A sharp frown flashed across Mikhail's face, and it seemed he had not realized her aunt would try to pressure her publicly.

But had that not been his intention when he arrived with her aunt?

The anger and hurt stabbing Payton's heart was potent. Why was it so difficult for the people who claimed to love her to respect her right to live life the way she wanted?

She pulled her hand from his, without acknowledging his generosity with a curtsy. Meeting the eyes of her aunt, Payton let the anger burn in her gaze, and Aunt Florence had the grace to blush.

She looked to Mikhail, and the cold determination was unmistakable in his eyes.

Then Payton turned away. She would be flayed for ignoring a prince, but she cared not what he or anyone thought.

She would only be encouraged by the desires in her heart.

Payton cut Mikhail dead, and pure pride swelled in his chest. He threw back his head and laughed, loving her fire, uncaring of the shocked murmurs rippling through the ballroom.

Her steps faltered at his obvious amusement, and she twisted her head and met his gaze with a fierce glare. And he was so damned glad to see it was not one of pain. Ecstasy as if she were kissing him tingled up his spine, when her lips quirked and humor flashed deep in her golden gaze. She had not reacted from a place of hurt or deliberate spitefulness, but from a place of refusing to bow to the dictates of her family and society.

He grabbed a glass from a passing footman and raised it in her direction.

There were several gasps behind him which he ignored.

Dance with me, he mouthed, and her eyes widened, that irresistible smile he loved so much curved into her lips. Then sadness suffused her face. It pained him to see it.

Mikhail's world shifted when she moved toward him.

A waltz started, and he drew her into his arms. "Thank you."

"I have selfish reasons," she said with a somber smile. "I know you dislike scandal, and I would not have you endure one because of my actions. I would prefer us to part amicably than with anger."

She cared. "Thank you, Payton. You honor me."

She arched an elegant brow. "I also love dancing, and it has been months since I had the pleasure, aside from our last ball."

The unspoken words hinted of a society that had made no effort to forgive and accept.

He drew her a bit closer than what was considered appropriate and heat flared in her gaze, then she lowered her lashes, hiding from him. "Then I will dance all night with you."

Her cheeks flushed becomingly. "Are you saying you are now comfortable with my touch?" She flexed her fingers on his shoulders.

"More so than I have ever been."

Doubt clouded her gaze. It was not enough for him to say the words. He would have to show her. He tightened his grip and spun her with dizzying swirls, wishing he could wipe the evident heartbreak from her eyes.

Tonight.

He would wait no longer. He must know if he was capable of accepting all she had to offer, and he would act tonight.

Payton released Mikhail's hands, curtsied, and walked away.

"*They have danced six dances now,*" a voice filled with shock and what sounded like admiration said.

"*It is scandalous, that is what it is!*"

"*I think she is an original.*"

This time the notes of admiration were filled with warmth.

"*I would say the Duke of Avondale has clearly declared who will be his duchess.*"

This tone was filled with envy.

Payton did not care. She could feel Mikhail's eyes on her; the swell of the gossip murmurings rose, but she was becoming immune to it all. It was freeing to know how little she cared for their opinion in this moment.

"Payton!" The sharp call of her aunt did not deter her, and pure pleasure wrapped itself around her heart as she ignored the head of her family.

She met the eyes of Connie, and a full-blown smile burst on Payton's lips when the duchess raised her glass of champagne and gave her a mock bow. Payton winked, and Connie laughed, and the ballroom throng witnessed the byplay.

Payton swept from the ballroom to the foyer, ignoring those who tried to signal her attention. She was one of the first guests to depart, and it took little effort for her carriage to be brought around.

She waited until she was settled inside before releasing the laugh she had been suppressing. This night had been perfect…almost. The freedom to act on her feelings had been so rewarding. When she had returned to his arms, uncaring of the world around for the first time she could ever remember, she had felt the crack in the belief she could never fit in his world.

She had soared in his arms, the desperate realization that while she did not want to be a part of the hypocrisy of high society, the easy condemnation and gossip, the desire to be Mikhail's wife, his lover, his princess and his duchess, had rattled in her head, a hammer to her resistance. And when she took the plunge, society would be the one that needed to fit into *her* world. A society where there was kindness to the wallflowers, where it was acceptable to invite the bluestocking to her balls, where the gent who possessed two left feet would still be encouraged to waltz, and, if it was her wish, to ride in Hyde Park astride in trousers. The very title she feared had the power for her to act however she wanted, if she would but have the strength to reach for him.

What about never knowing what it is like to touch him? How could she ever hope to defeat such demons?

There was a lurch, and she slipped a bit forward. A few minutes passed, and she stirred. Mayfair, where her father's town house was located, was not all that far from Connie's residence. They should have arrived by now. Payton lifted her head and frowned. Was it her imagination that the horses were moving faster? She banged on the carriage roof, and a few seconds later the portal slid open.

"Why have we increased our—?" *What?*

Dozens of men on horseback surrounded her carriage, and the countryside they raced past was not familiar in the least. Pulling the watch from her pelisse, she gaped at the time. She had been woolgathering for almost an hour.

Fear slithered along her spine. "Stop the carriage," she ordered, her mind churning with confusion and determination.

Why would the driver detour without informing her? She gasped when a horse trotted alongside the equipage, and she identified Vladimir. She opened the window. "What are you doing? Please order the driver to stop at once."

"Will you leave the carriage in the middle of nowhere?"

She glared at him. "What is the meaning of this?"

A slight smile quirked his lips. "I am being allowed to atone for my stupidity."

"By kidnapping me?" For the most awful precious seconds she had thought it could have been Lord Jensen, and she would have to endure a similar fate as Phillipa had when a man who had been obsessed kidnapped her.

Relief pulsed inside, and then a thought occurred. "Are you planning to do away with me for Princess Tatiana?"

Shock flared wide in Vladimir's eyes to be quickly replaced by amusement.

"No, Miss Peppiwell. Please be assured you have nothing to fear."

"I am not sure how things are done in Russia, but kidnapping here is a punishable crime."

The dratted man's lips twitched.

"I am taking you to Kent at Prince Alexander's

command."

Payton spluttered at the man's gall. She slammed the window shut and tried to settle her thoughts. She rocked with the motion of the carriage with a steady sense of anticipation building inside her. Mikhail was being outrageous and so improper. A smile tugged at her lips. She did not want to even imagine the gossip there would be if this got out.

Payton was infuriated. Mikhail really had the temerity to have the bounder Vladimir kidnap her. Was he aware the depth of scandal it could cause if it were ever discovered?

Now, approximately two hours after she had left the ball in London, that he delivered her to one of the most glorious castles she had ever seen, did not detract from his outrageous action. The outriders had broken away from the carriage once the horses trotted into the driveway. Payton descended the carriage to be received by the servants awaiting her arrival.

She felt mystified. The head housekeeper, Mrs. Claxon, took charge in quick order, and introduced Payton to the line of staff, then ushered her inside before escorting her upstairs to the loveliest of chambers, where an elegant maid modestly curtsied, awaiting her orders.

Her cheeks burned. What must they be thinking? Only a woman of loose morals would be at the prince's house at such a late hour, unaccompanied, yet they treated her with the utmost respect and kindness.

The chamber was decorated in antique gold and blue, with six soaring windows facing the rolling expanse of the green castle grounds. A Parisian chaise lounge upholstered in golden silk stood in the far corner, and one of the most exquisite writing desks Payton had ever seen sat under the windows. She indulged in a bath to remove the sweat and dust of travel and dressed in a matching blue jacket and skirt trimmed in silver, and a soft peach shirt with ruffled sleeves that had been laid out. Payton did not question how her valise had been delivered along with her to the castle.

It seemed he had planned this with great thoroughness.

She marched to the oak armoire and wrenched the door opened. She had several day dresses, riding habits, and even a few ball gowns organized inside.

Good heavens. Did he not plan to return her home?

She stiffened her shoulders and exited the chamber. The majestic beauty of the castle took Payton's breath away. She toured the lower rooms, seeking Mikhail in the parlor or drawing room. They were decorated in ornate elegance; if the ceilings had not been so high, the mass of detail might have seemed fussy, but the proportions were splendid, and yet the castle seemed very lived-in and comfortable. The rooms were all decorated with elegant furniture in Italian marble and carved mahogany. The windows were covered with sweeping curtains in brocade velvet with the ducal shield displayed in gold braid on each of the tassel-festooned pelmets. The walls were hung with some of the most exquisite paintings she had ever seen. Payton doubted that even the British Museum held such great works of art. The chairs and sofas were upholstered in silk in muted shades of silver and blue in one room and in crimson and gold in the next.

Payton had never seen such a pleasing interior.

She searched for the library or an office, for she refused to believe he would bring her here and not be present. She came upon a room where a faint light shone beneath the door. She rapped on the door, and when no answer came, she opened it and entered.

It was a library. No—it was a world of fantasy and dreams where walls and walls of books rose in three stories of stunning splendor. It was the most magnificent library Payton had ever seen.

"This is so glorious," she gasped, unable to credit her eyes.

"This is one of the reasons I brought you here."

She muffled the squeak and spun sharply.

Good heavens.

Mikhail stood in the doorway, obviously having recently emerged from a bath. He was dressed in formal trousers and jacket, complemented by a blue waistcoat and an expertly tied silken cravat. His black hair was neatly groomed, although slightly damp, without a strand out of place, his blue eyes were cool and distant; he was every inch the aristocrat. Against her own volition she was intrigued by this side of him. This man seemed cold and arrogant…more like a duke or prince than her Mikhail. She was overwhelmingly conscious of how much she had missed him, when only hours before she had been in his arms waltzing.

She loved him utterly.

An unbearable tension wound itself around her heart with the admission.

She buried the flare of pleasure at seeing him and gave him a look of pure disgruntlement. "Did you believe seeing books would make me forgive your deplorable behavior? Disabuse yourself of the notion, Mik — your highness."

Regret flared in his eyes. "Please do not refer to me as such."

Her heart softened. "I won't if that is your wish."

"I see you have refreshed yourself?"

"Are we to ignore the elephant in the room?"

His lips twitched. "I do not understand your phrase."

"Very well, are you going to ignore the deplorable behavior I just mentioned?"

He grunted.

"You had me kidnapped."

Silence stretched between them for a moment.

"Escorted," he finally said.

She frowned. "To what end? You and I are — "

"Will you dine with me? Dinner will be served within the

next hour."

Oh. "I am not sure I can wait a full hour for you to tell me why you went through so much to bring me here."

"Maybe I wanted to show you just a bit of what you would be giving up. You would be mistress of all you survey."

She snorted and rolled her eyes. "You know I have no interest in your wealth."

A smile touched his lips.

Then another bout of terrible silence. They stood in the library simply staring at each other. Shadows of torment lingered in his eyes, and he tugged at the cravat at his throat. The nervous gesture made her heart ache.

"I would love to dine with you, Mikhail."

His eyes were cold, his expression icy. "I thank you."

So formal…so distant. Was now the time to tell him she loved him and wanted to be his wife? "Mikhail, I—"

"I will see you at seven."

"Please wait."

He fisted his hands at his side and then faced her. The powerful emotions in his eyes made her heart flip, but in a good way. "Tell me, please, why did you bring me here?"

"I am not able to let you go."

Was he saying he loved her?

His eyes never strayed from her face. "I already have all the wealth and connections I could possibly want. I do not need a marriage to provide me with more. I want a marriage with a woman who respects me, trusts me, desires me, and above all, loves me."

"I do," she said, walking toward him. "I love you."

For a heart-wrenching moment he did nothing. There was no reaction from his body or his eyes. And it petrified Payton. "Do you love me?"

"Yes." There was no hesitation in his voice.

Sweet relief crashed through her, but there was a dark

edge in his tone, and her heart squeezed in discomfort and slight fear. "You do not seem happy at the realization."

Without speaking he thumbed the latch on the door and leaned against the wooden frame. His penetrating stare never wavered. "I know I adore you. The utter wonder of meeting you and knowing you have taken a piece of my heart, although I've only known you for seven days, has not escaped me. I do not need seven weeks or seven years to know you are the woman for me, Payton. I know it now. I see it in your smiles, your kisses, the passion and joy you find in the simple pleasures of life. What I see I admire, and I can only grow to love and appreciate you more. And it is because I feel such a need for you, I would prefer to release you rather than bind you to a life of pain and unhappiness."

Fear, cold and dreadful, slithered through her, alarming in its extremity. "I do not fear your world." She pushed past the lump in her throat. "The doubts are still there, and they may never leave, but I do not care. I want what you want, Mikhail. I want to be your lover, your friend, the woman you turn to when your nights are cold with nightmares, when you want to share a humorous anecdote, the person you turn to when you are angry and simply need to moan, the woman you want to have children with. I would desire this with you, even if you were a simple farmer. I want to marry you, and if I falter in the privileged world in which we will live, then I will make use of the power in the titles you so generously bestow."

"And if I never allow your touch?"

She flinched subtly, and his eyes sharpened.

"I do not believe it will be so."

He pushed from the door and slowly shrugged out of his jacket, then his waistcoat and shirt. She remained speechless as he removed his trousers, his unmentionables, and shoes, until he stood gloriously naked. Her breath caught at the sight of him, and her pulse started to hammer.

Payton closed her eyes for precious seconds and then snapped them open. Mikhail was still standing there, his body perfectly chiseled, with an arrogant tilt of his head. But his eyes… *Oh,* they glowed with fear, determination, lust, and love.

He prowled over to where she stood rooted, all sinewy grace and power.

"I submit myself to your touch," he said, his voice darker than the shades of midnight and sin.

His meaning rocketed through her. *No,* her mind screamed even as she lifted a finger and glided it over the hardened flesh of his chest with the lightest of caresses.

What if he allowed her touch and realized he could never want such intimacy with her?

"Touch me," he invited.

She pressed firmer, and he sucked in a breath on a sharp hiss, and she dropped her hands.

Payton lifted her eyes to his. "You honor me with such trust, Mikhail, but it is not needed. I can see the torment in your gaze, and it would ravage me to cause you more pain. I will marry you, and I will be patient, because I believe in the trust and love you have in me, and we will eventually entwine ourselves around each other and shout from the joy and relief of sliding skin against skin. But it will not be this day…and I am content."

A shudder passed through him, and he pressed a soft kiss to her lips. "I need to know I can bear your touch, even if only for a few minutes. I feel no hope, and I cannot suffer to see the pain in your eyes when I flinch from you. It is dull now, but it will only grow, until you start to hate me, until you will be forced to turn to another for something I can never give you."

She gasped. "This is what you believe of me?"

"No…I can see the woman you are. I see your strength and honor, and the capability for love and forgiveness. But

I would not bind us together with even the possibility that I may never be able to bear your touch." He crouched with an animalistic grace and swiped his cravat from the parquet floor.

"Bind me...touch me."

Bind him? The idea was so deliciously shocking and wicked, a pulse of wanton heat throbbed between her folds.

He strolled and sank into the chair by the fire, and he was so beautiful he took Payton's breath.

The trust he placed in her was enormous; it humbled her and filled her with fierce pride and love. He was doing this for *her*. Facing the demons of nightmares past because he did not want to see her unhappy.

She would treasure such a trust.

Acting on instincts she began to remove her clothes, strolling over to him and accepting his aid to remove her laces and buttons. Then she, too, was unashamedly naked. A pleased smile curved her lips as his heavy-lidded gaze of appreciation roamed over her body. She purred deep in her throat as the thick length of his erection flexed eagerly.

The broad width of the high winged-back chair made it impossible to bind his hands behind him. Instead, she rent her shift and used the strips to tie each of his hands to the armchair. Payton was very conscious that with each touch, he tensed, and he visibly forced himself to relax.

She leaned in, her breast close to his mouth and whispered, "If you want me to stop...call me Myrtle." His brow lifted, and she straightened and dipped into a slight curtsy. "Miss Payton Myrtle Peppiwell at your command, my prince."

His fingers gripped the arm of the chair, a growl bursting free of his mouth. "Touch me," he urged, blue fire of need sparking in his eyes. "Take me."

And God help her, she did, desperately wanting to experience the sweet burn of him sliding into her, possessing her body and heart, and knowing he bore her touch…even if it was fleeting.

Mikhail trembled when she pressed the flat of her palm against his chest right above his pounding heart, the first such direct contact in years.

Payton's touch was fire and ice.

Pain and pleasure.

Dread and exquisite torment.

Myrtle.

From the amusement twisting her lips, no doubt she believed it was an unattractive name. But everything about her captivated Mikhail. He flinched, and she froze. Yet when she removed her palm he felt bereft.

"Use your lips on me." The command snapped from him almost against his own volition, but he had imagined too many times how the flick of her tongue would feel.

She leaned forward and licked the very place her hand had been resting. Fire streaked through him, and his stomach roiled.

He gritted his teeth, tipping back his head as memories of dozens of hands pinched and whipped his skin, biting and licking, forcing him to feel pleasure from their depravity.

"Look at me." Her calm soothing voice was a relief, and he snapped his eyes opened, directing his sole attention to Payton.

The hum of memory receded, and all he could see was her.

"Do not look away from me," she said softly, her eyes devouring him.

The pleasure she took in looking at him sent a thrill shooting through his heart.

"I want to kiss you."

"Yes," he growled.

A shy but wanton smile graced her lips. She stroked her fingers through his hair, acclimating him to her touch. "But not on your lips…everywhere but your lips." She stroked her fingers down over the sharp angles of his jaw, down over his shoulders, tenderly.

With tentative grace, she climbed into his lap. Everything in him shut down, and he braced himself for the revulsion. It never came. All he could feel was the softness of her ass as she wiggled against his thighs, her scent—spiced wine and berries enveloped his nose—and her soft husky voice murmuring soothing nonsense. He was surrounded by Payton, and all he could feel and anticipate was *her*.

She shifted so she sat on his lap, her legs bracketing his, opening her pink womanly flesh to his eyes.

Christ.

"The first time I heard your voice, without even seeing your face, I wanted to be ridden by you desperately hard."

She slipped her hands around his neck and leaned in so her wonderful breasts were pressed against his chest.

Mikhail groaned.

"I will happily oblige you," she drawled. "But first I am going to lick and taste you all over."

And she did. With soft swipes of her hot tongue across his chest, over his nipples, and down. To then come back up in a torturous journey of slow kisses. He felt as if he were enslaved to the stroke of her tongue, desperately wanting her to go lower and lower until she kissed his length.

"God, you're beautiful."

A secret smile tugged at her lips at his praise, and she shimmied from his lap and knelt in front of him.

"Payton, I—"

She enveloped him in fire.

A ragged groan burst from his throat.

God, he'd wanted to feel Payton's mouth all over his body for the longest time. In the dark corners of his heart, he'd dreamed of having those arrestingly alluring full lips wrapped around him, taking him with the innocent hunger he could see blazing in her golden orbs. But the fantasy was nothing like the reality. She licked and sucked his cock beautifully, and with wicked carnality. It was the most erotic thing Mikhail had ever seen, her lips stretching over his cock, her tongue flicking and curling over its engorged head as she knelt before him.

Rip. The shift tore against his straining arms, and he trembled under the devastating pleasure of her touch. Her mouth stretched over his cock, her cheeks hollowing as she drew on him, her eyes never leaving his. Her lips made him harder than he'd ever been. He thrust slowly and deeply into her mouth, loving the sounds she made—soft purrs of pleasure.

As her mouth loved him, Mikhail felt as if he were going mad from the hunger clawing through his body. His head fell back against the cushions of the chair, and groan slipped from him as she licked from his balls to the tip of his cock. He could wait no longer to be inside her.

"Straddle my lap," he growled, his voice so guttural with arousal he sounded unintelligible.

She complied, sliding against his thigh, and he hissed at the wetness he felt.

"Lift your breasts and bring them to my mouth."

She moaned, gripping his length and positioning him against the entrance of her body.

"Payton." Her name was a plea of raw need.

Rip.

His hands burst free; her eyes widened as he pounced. Gripping her long tresses, he pulled her down to him with sensual intent, drawing her so that she straddled him on the chair, her knees bracketing his hips.

"Mikhail!" She cried his name as he pushed his hand between her legs and sent three fingers delving deep. She was wet, so damn wet. She twisted and arched to him as he trailed his tongue down her neck to her breasts. He lurched from the chair, and in two strides he was lowering her onto the sofa, notching the head of his cock at her entrance. She screamed when he plunged deep inside the clenching depths of her heat.

He kissed her fiercely, capturing her cries, and thrust into her hard with deep measured strokes. He groaned into their kiss as she pushed her hands low and gripped his ass.

Merciful Christ!

She moved in urgent counterpoint to his fierce thrust, giving him everything he demanded and more.

"Let me hear it," he whispered roughly. "Say the words."

"I love you."

He went to his knees, gripped her thighs, and pulled her to the edge of the sofa. She tilted her hips, drawing her feet up until they rested on the sofa's edge, opening her core to his thrusts. He lost himself in her, in her cries, in her wet heat, and the peace he felt being inside of her almost scared him. The smacking and sounds of their loving drowned him in sensuality, and his cravings deepened. Never had a woman made him this damned hungry. She begged for more, and he obliged. He gripped her hips as he began to hammer into her with quick deep strokes that sent pleasure rippling from his spine to his brain and back down to his balls. He couldn't speak. Couldn't praise her or encourage her to milk his cock.

He could only feel.

Never had he immersed himself so completely into making love, never had he felt such primitive need, shattering all barriers of caution he'd normally possessed.

She burned him alive.

He speared his fingers through her hair, anchoring her

gaze to his. "I love you, Payton."

She clamped down on his length and bit into his shoulder as she convulsed, hoarse moans ripping from her. She hugged him and wrapped her legs high around the middle of his back, and he cradled her buttocks in his palms as he tilted her hips, shafting deeper and deeper with each stroke. He felt consumed, overwhelmed, and shockingly hungry for more.

She dug her fingernails into his shoulders. "I ache...I burn, but please do not stop," she gasped, trembling as ecstasy seized her, and she rippled over his cock, bathing him in her pleasure.

Fire raced along his nerve endings as he emptied deep inside her.

And he tumbled into a peace and contentment he had never felt in his life.

He rolled with her, placing her still-quaking body on top of his. Her tremors subsided, and he tightened his arms around her, stroking her hair.

"Will you marry me?"

A sweet chuckle spilled from her. "Oh yes."

And he was completed.

Epilogue

Payton cut the corner at breakneck speed. Her love thundered behind her on his horse, but the power of Aeton made it possible for her to stave off Sage. A few seconds later they slowed the horses to a canter, and she giggled at the disgruntled look on Mikhail's face.

His lips curved in a smile. "You minx, you cheated."

She tossed back her head. "Absolutely not. I simply said I cannot wait for you to bind me to the bed later tonight and have your delightfully wicked way with me. *You* were distracted, and I simply rode away."

He nudged his horse closer, and she reached out and clasped his hand. Though he welcomed more and more of her touch since marrying two weeks ago, Payton insisted they indulge in bed play where he was in complete control and she was at his wonderful mercy. She'd suspected they would forever have that aspect of absolute restraint when making love in their life, but she did not mind it. In fact, she hungered for the eroticism of the more unusual part of being with him and trusted him wholly with her pleasure.

If society was shocked they had married so quickly and in a small ceremony at Sherring Cross's chapel, Payton did not know. They had buried themselves in the country, basking in each other and refusing all invitations to balls, houses parties, and soirees. They had only journeyed to London two days past to assist her sister Phoebe in preparing for the upcoming season in a few weeks' time. Payton would help sponsor Phoebe into society, and be there to guide her through the murky waters. Parliament would also open, and Mikhail would take his seat.

Their presence had been met with speculation and something akin to awe, and a bevy of callers had already descended on their town house. Much to the dismay of the *haute monde*, they were not yet available to callers.

"*It's Prince Alexander and Princess Payton.*"

At their names, she glanced in the direction of the other riders on Rotten Row in Hyde Park.

"*She is wearing trousers!*"

"*Outrageous.*"

Mikhail winked, and she chortled.

Life was wonderful.

Acknowledgments

I thank God every day for allowing me to find my passion.

To my husband, thank you for being my biggest fan and supporter, and for loving the fact that I am a ninja in disguise. Also for reading all my drafts and listening to me plot ideas at three a.m.! You are so damn wonderful.

Thank you to my amazing editor, Alycia Tornetta, for shaping *The Royal Conquest* into a gem!

To my wonderful readers, thank you for picking up my book and giving me a chance! You guys rock! Special shout out to my Rioters. Just hanging with you guys, talking books, *The Walking Dead*, and *Banshee* keeps me sane! Thank you.

Special THANK YOU to everyone that leaves a review, bloggers, fans, friends…I have always said reviews to authors are like a pot of gold to Leprechauns. Thank you all for adding to my rainbow one review at a time.

About the Author

I am an avid reader of novels with a deep passion for writing. I especially love romance and enjoy writing about people falling in love. I live a lot in the worlds I create and I actively speak to my characters (out loud). I have a warrior way "Never give up on my dream." When I am not writing, I spend a copious amount of time drooling over Rick Grimes from *The Walking Dead*, Lucas Hood from *Banshee*, watching Japanese Anime and playing video games with my love—Dusean. I also have a horrible weakness for ice cream.

I am always happy to hear from readers and would love for you to connect with me via Website | Facebook | Twitter

To be the first to hear about my new releases, get cover reveals and excerpts you won't find anywhere else, sign up for my Newsletter.

Happy reading!

Don't miss out on more Scandalous romance...

SEDUCING THE MARQUESS

a *Lords and Ladies in Love* novel by Callie Hutton

Richard, the Marquess of Devon is satisfied with his ton marriage. His wife of five months, Lady Eugenia Devon wants her very proper husband to fall in love with her. After finding a naughty book, she begins a campaign to change the rules. Her much changed and decidedly wicked behavior drives her husband to wonder if his perfect Lady has taken a lover. But the only man Eugenia wants is her husband. The book can bring sizzling desire to the marriage or cause an explosion.

PORTRAIT OF A FORBIDDEN LADY

a *Those Magnificent Malverns* novel by Kathleen Bittner Roth

Lady Georgiana Cressington is living a nightmare. Her forced return to Summerfield Hall reunites her with the man she once loved, yet betrayed. Sir Robert Garreck, knighted by the queen, lives in a mansion near the family estate Georgiana's father won in a crooked card game. Despite Georgiana's devastating duplicity, Rob never stopped loving his forbidden lady. Facing danger and a long-hidden truth, Georgiana and Rob try to claim the powerful love hey once had.

Made in United States
North Haven, CT
28 December 2021

13783624R00136